Courtney Hewitt thinks of herself as an ordinary girl. She likes music. Movies. Hanging with her friends. Most of all, she likes having a good time.

Then everything goes nuts. Countries lob misslies at each other. Bombs fall. Chemical weapons are unleashed.

Say goodbye to ordinary.

Now her life is an unending nightmare. Danger is everywhere. To survive, she must do things she never imagined doing. She must reach deep inside herself and be as tough as she can be---or be as dead as the millions who have already died.

OBLIVION.....OR LIFE. WHICH WILL IT BE?

Books by David Robbins

ENDWORLD Universe
ENDWORLD
WILDERNESS
WHITE APACHE   BLOOD FEUD
A GIRL, THE END OF THE WORLD AND EVERYTHING

Series
ANGEL U
DAVY CROCKETT

Horror
PRANK NIGHT   SPOOK NIGHT
HELL-O-WEEN   THE WERELING
THE WRATH   SPECTRE

Novels
HIT RADIO   BLOOD CULT

Westerns
GUNS ON THE PRAIRIE   THUNDER VALLEY
RIDE TO VALOR   TOWN TAMERS
BADLANDERS   DIABLO
THE RETURN OF THE VIRGINIAN

Movie Novelizations
MEN OF HONOR   PROOF OF LIFE
TWISTED

Nonfiction
HEAVYE TRAFFIC
(A history of the DEA)

A GIRL, A DOG, AND ZOMBIES ON THE MUNCH

David Robbins

Copyright © 2018 David Robbins

All rights reserved. No part of this publication may be reproduced,
distributed, transmitted in any form
or introduced into a retrieval system, by any means,
(electronic,mechanical, photocopying, recording or otherwise) without
the prior written permission of the author, except in the case of brief
quotations embodied in critical reviews and certain other noncommercial
uses
permitted by copyright law.

Any such distributions or reproductions of this publication will be
punishable under the United Squays Copyright Act and the Digital
Millennium Copyright Act to the fullest extent including Profit Damages
(SEC 504 A1), Statutory Damages (SEC 504 2C) and Attorney Fees and
Court Costs.

DISCLAIMER: This is a fictional work. Names, characters, places and
incidents either are the product of the author's imagination or are used
fictitiously and any resemblance to actual persons, living or dead,
business establishments, events or locales is entirely coincidental.

Published by Mad Hornet Pub.
Printed in the United Squays of America
ISBN: 978-1-950096-02-2

Dedicated to Judy,
Joshua and Shane

CHAPTER 1

The end of the world sucked.

Courtney Hewitt glared at the ugly clouds that filled the sky from horizon to horizon, then at the darkly sinister countryside to either side, and finally at the man leading their little group.

Were it up to her, she would be safe and cozy in her room in Minneapolis watching videos or talking on the phone or any of the other hundred and one things she used to like to do.

The last thing she would ever want to be doing was hiking through the boonies, bound for the north part of Minnesota in the hope that there might be a safe haven from the madness.

Was it only days ago, Courtney reflected, that she had been in high school? Only days ago that her life had been ordinary and peaceful? Even if she hadn't realized how sweet that was at the time?

She missed being able to take a shower---dear God, how she missed that!---and not having to worry where her next meal would come from.

And---the biggie---not having to worry about being killed.

A sharp growl from a stand of trees to her left brought Courtney up short.

The others stopped, too.

Their leader, if you could call him that, was Alex Dutfeld, the father of one of her best friends, Sally Ann, who was right behind her. Sally Ann was one of the brainiest people in school. And one of the nicest.

Her father, however, was an alcoholic, and at the moment he was savoring another mouthful from a silver flask. In his other hand he gripped a Remington pistol-grip shotgun. Wedged under his belt was a Ruger Vaquero.

Sally Ann sighed. "Look at him," she said bitterly. "He's half soused."

"I'd be more worried about that growl," Courtney said.

No sooner were the words out of her mouth than an apparition shuffled out of the trees toward them.

Once, it had been human. A young woman, not much older than Courtney and Sally Ann, her blonde hair filthy, her face a horrible mask of decomposed flesh. Her eyes were glazed and empty of life, yet there she was, lurching toward them as if animated by a force from beyond the grave. As she advanced, she clacked her teeth in anticipation of feasting on their flesh.

"Another damn zombie," said the fourth member of their party, and Billy Thompson, another of Courtney's friends from high school, moved between them and the new threat. He was limping from an injury he suffered in the Twin Cities.

"You need a weapon," Sally said. "We all do."

"Blame him," Billy said, with a jerk of his head toward her father. "He took all the guns, remember?"

Courtney remembered it all too well. Mad because they wouldn't do as he wanted, Alex Dutfeld had taken command. As the oldest, Alex felt he should be calling the shots.

"What are you three muttering about?" Alex said as

he capped his flask.

Billy pointed at the zombie, now less than twenty feet away. "Do something."

"As slow as that thing's moving?" Alex said, and shook his head. "It'd be a waste of ammo. Kill it yourself, boy. You're supposed to be the great high school jock, aren't you?"

Balling his fist and glowering, Billy took a half-step toward the older man.

Sally Ann quickly whispered, "Please don't provoke him, Billy."

Courtney was the only one still watching the zombie. Casting about, she spied a rock about the size of a cantaloupe and scooped it up.

Just as the female zombie put on a burst of speed.

Another growl rent the air. But this time it wasn't the zombie. It was Gaga, the mongrel Courtney had rescued in the Twin Cities. The usually timid dog sprang at the zombie's legs and snapped viciously.

The zombie ignored her. Fingers curled like claws, it lunged at Billy, who jerked aside, swearing.

Serves you right, Courtney almost said out loud. He should have been paying attention. Instead, she took a bound and brought the rock crashing down on the zombie's head. Bone crunched and gore spattered, and the creature stiffened and stumbled.

Before Courtney could press her advantage, Billy tore the rock from her grasp and attacked the thing himself. As she had seen him do once before, he nearly went berserk. He smashed and pounded even after the zombie was down, hitting and hitting until its head was a puddle of crushed bone and mush. Finally he stopped, stepped back, gulped a few deep breaths, and faced Alex Dutfeld. "I want my gun back."

"Not going to happen," Alex said.

"I mean it," Billy said, taking a step and hefting the gore-spattered rock.

"Or what?" Alex taunted, and pointed the shotgun at Billy.

Courtney was about to intervene but Sally Ann beat her to it. Darting between her father and Billy, she held out her hands toward them.

"Stop it! Both of you! I'm so tired of this bickering." She faced her father. "Dad, you had no right to take all the guns. If you're not going to protect us, you should give them back."

"Not going to happen, baby girl," Alex said.

"Stop calling me that," Sally Ann snapped. "I've asked you a thousand times. I'm not a baby anymore."

"I held you in my arms when you were born," Alex said. "You'll always be my baby girl to me."

"I want my revolver," Billy said.

"Yours, hell," Alex said. "You found it it in somebody's house."

"I'm so tired of you," Billy said.

"Works both ways, kid," Alex said.

Afraid their argument would escalate, Courtney spoke up. "We can settle this later. Right now, we have the zombies to worry about. "

"She's right," Sally Ann said. "We're out in the open. Exposed. Let's find somewhere to rest a while."

"We'll move on when he drops that rock," Alex said, nodding at Billy.

"Billy?" Sally Ann said.

Billy glowered at Alex, the rock clutched tight.

"Billy?" Sally Ann said again.

"He'll get us killed, as drunk as he is," Billy said.

"Up yours, boy," Alex said.

Courtney put a hand on Billy's arm. "Please. For me."

Their eyes met, and Courtney felt, again, the deep well of affection he bore for her. He'd admitted as much not long ago, much to her surprise. They had been friends forever. It never occurred to her that he might care for her more than that.

Billy's fingers loosened and the rock thudded to the ground.

"Smart," Alex said, and laughed.

"Dad!" Sally Ann said.

Alex resumed hiking. "There's a farm yonder," he said, pointing. "We'll stop there. Maybe find something to eat."

Courtney and Sally Ann and Billy let Alex get a little ahead before they continued on.

"I can't take much more of him," Billy said so only they would hear.

"He's my dad," Sally Ann said.

"So we're supposed to go on letting him boss us around?" Billy responded.

Courtney saw Alex glance back. "Now's not the time for this," she whispered. "We'll talk later. In the meantime, there's the farmhouse. I could use a hot meal."

"I hear that," Sally Ann said.

Courtney shifted her backpack to better distribute the weight. The left strap kept digging into her shoulder.

Billy whispered, "We really have to do something about Sally's old man."

"Let it drop, I told you," Courtney said. "We'll deal with him later."

"Deal how?" Billy said. "Ask him pretty please to give back the revolver he took from me?"

"For the love of God," Courtney said. "Give it a rest."

"We should ditch him," Billy ignored her. "Wait our chance and slip away."

"Without weapons?"

"We'll find new ones."

Courtney was looking down at the road but now she raised her head---just in time to keep from bumping into Sally Ann. Her friend had stopped and was staring at the farmhouse.

So was her father.

The reason was obvious.

Three stories high, with a peaked roof and a weathervane, the house was yellow with white trim. The first and second floors were fitted with four windows to a side. The third floor had a small window near the peak. And there, as plain as anything, glowed a light.

"A lantern, I bet," Sally Ann said.

"Or a propane lamp," Billy said.

"It means somebody is living there," Alex said. "It means we have to be extra careful."

"You can't go marching up waving the shotgun," Sally Ann said. "They won't let us in."

"Maybe we should pass it by," Courtney said. "Find a place that's empty."

"The next farm could be miles away," Alex said. "I say we invite ourselves in."

"Those people might not want visitors," Courtney

said.

Alex made a clucking sound. "Haven't you been paying attention, Hewitt? World War Three has broken out. It's everyone for themself. Survival of the fittest, like in caveman times."

"We're not cavemen, dad," Sally Ann said. "We're civilized."

"Tell that to the bombs and missiles that rained down," Alex said. "Wake up and smell the blood, baby girl. Now let's go introduce ourselves."

CHAPTER 2

Courtney wasn't about to let Alex Dutfeld hurt innocent people. She had kept her temper in check and tried to be reasonable. And Alex was still being a douche.

As they neared the farmhouse, she walked faster and overtook him. He was so intent on the farmhouse, he didn't notice her until she passed him.

Gaga, as usual, was glued to her legs.

"What do you think you're doing?" Alex demanded.

Without looking back at him, Courtney said, "What decent people do. I'm going up to their front door and knock."

"Like hell you are," Alex said.

"Unless you're willing to shoot me in the back, watch me." Courtney tensed, the skin between her shoulderblades prickling, half-expecting him to actually shoot. He must have raised the shotgun because Sally Ann suddenly let out a sharp cry.

"Dad! Don't even think it!"

Courtney kept on walking. "You can cover me if you want, Alex." She added, "If you're sober enough." That last would get his goat.

Alex liked to boast that he could drink like a fish without any effect. He was kidding himself. When he was soused, he turned into a giddy idiot---or became mean.

Courtney put him from her mind and concentrated

on the farm.

A red barn stood beyond the house, only part of it visible. There were half a dozen outbuildings, including one that Courtney took to be a chicken coop. There was a hog pen, too, but no sign of the hogs. An oak tree overspread a dog house, but no dog.

"Maybe you'll meet a new friend," Courtney said to Gaga, who looked up at her with those adoring eyes.

The clouds had grown darker, casting the farmhouse, and everything else, in somber shadow.

The light, though still glowed in the third floor window.

Courtney couldn't see anyone moving around up there but she had the feeling that she was being watched.

The road passed within a hundred feet of the front of the house. A large mailbox hung open, and empty.

The barn, the coop, the other buildings---there was no sign of anyone, anywhere.

Squaring her shoulders, Courtney started up a walk toward the front porch. An old-fashioned swing chair swayed slightly in the breeze, creaking now and then. A rocking chair sat in the far corner.

Courtney tried to ignore the pounding of her heart and plastered a smile on her face. When she was midway along the walk, she called out, "Hello? Is anyone home?"

There was no response from the house.

But from the barn came a loud crash. Even though the double doors hung open, inside was pitch black.

Courtney dreaded it would be another of the living dead, but nothing emerged.

Courtney wondered where all the farm animals had

gotten to. She was a city girl, but her parents had taken her to an uncle's farm a few times, and there were chickens and cows and geese and whatnot all over the place.

A possible answer occurred to her: a chemical cloud.

She witnessed them firsthand in Minneapolis. An incoming missile would strike, but instead of an explosion, it spewed a thick green fog or mist that rapidly spread. Soon it would resemble a green cloud. That was when it would start to move as if alive, to crawl across the land swallowing everyone and everything in its path.

Those it swallowed were either never seen again---dissolved alive, most people believed---or they were changed. Mutated. They emerged from the clouds covered with blisters and ravening to spill the blood of every living thing they encountered.

Courtney hoped to God a green cloud hadn't come rolling across the farm.

She was almost to the porch when a curtain hanging in a front window moved---as if someone had been looking out and darted from sight.

Cautiously climbing the steps, Courtney stepped to the door, and knocked. "Hello? Anyone home? I don't mean you any harm." She pressed her ear to the door. Was it her imagination, or did she hear the scuffle of hurried footsteps?

"Hello! We'd very much like something to eat and drink if you can spare it."

The silence gnawed at her nerves.

Moving to the end of the porch she scanned the red barn and the coop and other buildings.

Nothing.

Courtney returned to the door and knocked louder. She tried the knob but it was locked. Jiggling it, she "Please! Open up, will you?:"

Over at the barn, something let out a bellow of rage and pain---and from its depths lumbered a monster.

Courtney stepped to the rail for a better view.

Once, it had been a bull. A huge black bull with horns that curved up and out. Sores and blisters covered its entire body, while green mucous oozed from its nose and mouth. Its eyes were red-rimmed furnaces of simmering fury. Snorting, it tore at the ground with a front hoof and glared about.

Courtney froze. She hoped that the bull would go back in the barn. But no. It was staring toward the front yard.

Courtney risked a glance and was racked by dismay. "No!" she gasped.

Sally Ann, her father, and Billy were out near the mailbox. Sally Ann and Billy recognized the danger and were imitating statues.

Not Alex. He was drinking from his flask. He raised it to his mouth, lowered it, and raised it again, not seeming to care that the bull could see them.

"You fool," Courtney whispered.

Sally Ann glanced at her father and said something and he laughed and took a few steps to one side and helped himself to another swig.

The bull uttered another fierce bellow and tore at the ground, all the while shaking its huge head from side to side.

Incredibly, Alex Dutfeld still didn't seem to realize the peril he was in. Capping the flask, he slid it into a pocket, then gestured with the Remington shotgun.

"You want some of this?" he taunted.

Courtney couldn't believe anyone could be so stupid. Maybe it was the alcohol. Or maybe it was just the fact that Alex had never possessed much common sense.

The bull charged.

"Dad, run!" Sally Ann cried, and tried to go to him but Billy wrapped his arms around her and held fast.

As for Alex, he was smiling and acting as if he didn't have a care in the world. Taking another couple of steps, he raised the shotgun.

Head down, spewing goo from both nostrils, the bull was a living locomotive. It covered the ground amazingly quick.

By Courtney's reckoning, about fifty feet separated them when Alex fired. The 12 gauge boomed and bucked and he scored a hit.

The bull stumbled, recovered, and resumed its charge.

Alex pumped the slide to feed a new shell into the chamber. He centered and fired and this time the bull pitched onto its front knees but it was instantly up again, its legs pumping. Alex worked the slide and fired a third time. He shot at the bull's head.

This time the bull barely slowed.

Courtney recalled that the Remington held four rounds. Alex was down to his last shell.

Grimly, Alex Dutfeld set himself and took deliberate aim. By now the bull was less than ten feet away. Alex fired and the bull reacted as if it had slammed into a wall. But it didn't drop. Lunging, the pus-spattered monstrosity hooked its head up and in.

Alex Dutfeld was caught flat-footed. The horn sheared into his chest like a hot knife into butter and he was lifted bodily into the air and shaken as a cat might shake a mouse. He opened his mouth to scream but only blood came out.

Sally Ann screamed, though. A piercing, hair-raising scream torn from her very soul. She would have run to him if not for the hold Billy had on her.

Courtney flew off the porch to go to their aid. She didn't know what she could possibly do but they were her friends.

The bull gave another toss of it head and Alex's limp body slid off the blood-drenched horn and plopped to the ground. It took a step toward Sally Ann and Billy, and staggered. It tried another step, and staggered worse. A loud snort, and the monster collapsed.

Billy let go of Sally Ann and she rushed to her father.

Courtney didn't take her eyes off the bull. Its tongue, lathered in mucous, hung from the side of its open mouth. She wasn't convinced it was dead until she stepped around to where she could see its head. The left eye was gone, the socket blown away. The left nostril, too. Other jagged holes brimmed with green fluid.

Sally Ann was bent over her dad, weeping. "No, no, no," she choked out.

Courtney had no idea where her own dad---and mom and brother and sister---had gotten to. She hadn't seen them since the war broke out. Feeling deep sympathy for Sally Ann's loss, Courtney put a hand on her friend's shoulder.

Billy picked up the shotgun. He jacked the slide, saw it was empty, and came over. Bending, he reached for the bandoleer around Alex's waist.

Courtney grabbed his wrist and shook her head. She

was about to say it wasn't the right time when they both heard a noise from the direction of the farmhouse.

The front door was opening.

CHAPTER 3

"Sally Ann!" Courtney said to warn her, but her friend was too overcome by grief to pay attention.

Billy glanced anxiously about and suddenly darted to where the Ruger revolver had fallen when Alex was struck by the bull. Snatching it off the ground, he spun toward the farmhouse.

A face appeared, low down. A pale, oval face framed by stringy brown hair.

"It's a little girl!" Courtney exclaimed.

The girl stood there, mired in shadow. She showed no emotion. She didn't call out or beckon.

"Why doesn't she say something?" Billy said. "Is she scared?"

"Wouldn't you be?" Courtney said. Smiling and holding her arms out from her sides, she said, "Hi there! We're friendly! Who are you? Are your parents home?"

The girl just looked at them.

"What's the matter with her?" Billy said.

"Hello? The end of the world as we know it." Courtney shook her head at how dense he could be. "Duh."

"That's not what I meant," Billy said. "Maybe it's the gun." He shifted the Vaquero behind his back and waved with his other hand. "Come on out where we can see you!"

Instead, the girl stepped back and closed the door.

"Stay here," Billy said, and started toward the house.

Courtney had always been quick on her feet. She caught up to him before he took three steps and snagged his wrist. "Use that head of yours, will you?"

"What?" Billy said in confusion. "What did I do now?"

"It's a little girl," Courtney reminded him. "She'll respond better to me than some strange man who goes barging in."

"Oh." Billy nodded. "That makes sense. But you shouldn't go in alone."

"Someone has to stay with Sally Ann."

Their friend was sprawled over her father, bawling uncontrollably.

"She'll be all right," Billy said.

Courtney stared.

"What?"

Courtney went on staring.

"All right. Fine," Billy said. "I'll stay with her. But anything goes down in there, you holler and I'll come running."

Courtney nodded and turned to go but now he grabbed her wrist.

"Take this," Billy said, and thrust the revolver at her.

"You might need it," Courtney said. "Other farm animals might have turned."

"I'll have the shotgun." Billy pushed the revolver into her hand. "Take this or I go with you. Sally Ann or no Sally Ann."

It was heavier than Courtney expected. Nickel plated---or so Alex once mentioned---with pearl grips and a six-inch barrel. If nothing else, she wryly thought, she could club a zombie to death with the thing.

Still, it was a weapon, and as much as she had disliked guns before the world went crazy, now they wouldn't last long without one.

Hiking her shirt, she tried sticking it under her belt but the gun was so heavy and her belt so thin, the revolver's weight threatened to pull her pants down to her knees.

By experimenting, she found that if she angled the barrel just right and slid it under her belt at the base of her spine, the revolver held snug between her and the backpack. And she could slide it out easy should she need to.

Courtney hurried to the farmhouse. The curtains remained undisturbed. Not really expecting a response, she knocked. She tried the knob. It was unlocked. She opened the door a couple of inches and said softly, "Little girl? Where are you?"

From deep in the house came a scratching sound that only lasted a few seconds.

"Little girl?"

Courtney pushed on the door. Without lights, it was hard to make things out. There was a sofa off to one side, pulled a couple of feet from the wall, and a chair the other way, and a fireplace along the far wall.

"Little girl? Please answer me."

Her hand on the revolver, Courtney edged inside. She went to call out and a foul odor assailed her, causing her to cough and nearly gag. Covering her mouth and nose with her hand, she ventured another couple of half-steps.

"My name is Courtney? Where are you?"

She heard the scratching again. From somewhere upstairs.

Every ounce of common sense she possessed urged her to wait for Billy and Sally Ann. But the thought of the little girl, alone and undoubtedly afraid, compelled her forward. She was almost to the middle of the room when a door at the far end of an adjoining hall swung wide and something appeared in the doorway---and hissed.

Courtney didn't waste an instant. Whirling, she dashed behind the sofa and crouched.

The glimpse she had of the silhouette of the thing showed it had been human. The hiss showed that it was now something else.

Listening for footsteps, Courtney scarcely breathed. Most zombies were slow and clumsy. Some, though, were frighteningly fast. Whichever, she was bound to hear it approach.

When over a minute went by and nothing happened, Courtney figured the thing had gone elsewhere. Playing it cautious, she raised her head above the back of the sofa.

Not six feet away stood a woman wearing a dress that was in tatters. She was covered with pus-oozing sores. Half the hair on her head was gone, and the hair that remained was a sickly yellowish-green. She glared about with eyes as red as blood.

Courtney turned to stone. The woman---the thing---was looking the other way. With any luck it would go back down the hall. But no. The creature moved to the front door, so quickly and so silently that if Courtney had blinked, she would have missed it.

Courtney didn't want to shoot if she could help it. These mutates, as Sally Ann had taken to calling them, were different from zombies. They were lethal horrors.

They went after anything and everything, and would as soon rip apart a dog or a cat as a person.

Undoubtedly, the poor woman had been caught in a chemical cloud, probably the same cloud that mutated the bull. She had been lucky in that she hadn't dissolved into nothingness. Why some people did while others were changed into hideous abominations, Courtney had no idea.

The creature was noisily sniffing the door. She bent to the knob and tried turning it but her hands wouldn't work right.

Courtney prayed she wouldn't get the door open. Billy and Sally Ann were out there, and would be attacked on sight.

Moving ever-so-slowly so as not to give herself away, Courtney extended the Vaquero. A shot to the head was all it would take. But she mustn't miss. The thing would be on her before she could get off another. She sighted down the barrel and put her thumb on the hammer to pull it back.

Courtney couldn't say what made her glance past the fireplace to where a flight of stairs led up to the second floor. Only the bottom few steps were visible, and a handrail. And there, her face pressed to the slats that supported the rail, was the little girl.

Courtney almost shouted for her to run. If the mutate saw her, the thing would be on her in a heartbeat.

The girl's features weren't all that clear, but Courtney had the impression the girl was staring at the woman in great sadness.

Then it hit her.

The woman was the little girl's mother.

Courtney's heart went out to the girl. She wanted to sneak over and get her out of there.

Just then the mutated mother turned toward the sofa and gave a sharp bark.

Courtney would have shrunk into the floor if she could. The thing had seen her but seemed surprised more than anything. She should shoot before it attacked but she couldn't with the little girl there. Not blow the girl's mother away in front of her.

The mutate tilted its head and sniffed, drops of pus dripping from its chin.

Please no, Courtney thought.

The creature snarled, and rushed at her.

Courtney fired. She hadn't used the Vaquero before or she would have held it tighter than she did. At the blast, the revolver whipped upward, jerking her arms. The shot intended to core the creature's head struck the woman in the neck, instead. Pus and gore sprayed all over. The mutate recoiled from the impact---and then came on again, its teeth bared in sheer savagery.

Courtney pointed the revolver and thumbed the hammer but she didn't have it all the way back when the creatue leaped onto the sofa and without missing a beat, sprang over it, slamming into Courtney and knocking her back against the wall. Steely fingers seized her wrists and teeth snapped at her neck.

Panic lent Courtney the strength to break loose and push the creature away but it only bought her a brief respite. With an guttural growl, the thing bit at Courtney's arm, at her shoulder.

Courtney swung the revolver, bashing the mutate across the face.

It had little effect.

The creature spread its jaws wide and went for Courtney's throat.

CHAPTER 4

Thrusting her elbow out, Courtney stopped the mutate's slavering jaws an inch from her skin. She felt its hot breath, smelled an awful reek.

"Mom, no!"

The shout from the little girl seemed to surprise the creature as much as it did Courtney. They both looked toward the girl, and Courtney's heart leaped in her chest.

The child had come around the bannister and stood with her eyes brimming with tears and her little fists clenched.

"Don't hurt her, mom! It's not right!"

The creature snarled.

Courtney found her voice. "Run!" she screamed. "This isn't your mother! Not anymore!"

The girl stood there.

With a roar worthy of a lion, the mutate started toward her.

Clinging fast with one hand, Courtney slammed her revolver against the creature's head. Once again her blow had no effect. The thing didn't even glance her way. It was only interested in the girl that had once been its daughter.

"Run!" Courtney screamed even as she jammed the Vaquero's muzzle against the creature's head behind its ear, and fired.

At the blast, part of the creature's skull exploded,

spewing hair and flesh and bone.

The thing managed a stiff-legged step, then collapsed.

Courtney let go and stepped back. She covered it, just in case, saying to the girl, "I'm sorry! I didn't have any choice! I couldn't let it hurt you!" She nudged the thing with her toe, half-afraid it might get back up.

Soft weeping filled the room.

Tears streaming down her cheeks, the girl came toward the prone figure, her hands outstretched.

"You shouldn't touch her," Courtney warned. "It might not be safe." There was no telling what contact with the pus could do.

The girl didn't seem to hear her. "Mommy," she said, and blinked tears away. "My mom!"

Courtney moved between them. "You shouldn't."

Her face glistening wet, the girl looked up. "My mom," she said yet again. Suddenly she threw her arms around Courtney's legs and bawled, her body shaking uncontrollably.

Courtney didn't know what to do. Her instinct was to lend comfort, but she didn't like the idea of standing in the middle of their living room when there might be more mutates around.

"I'm sorry for your loss, little one," Courtney said, patting the girl's shoulder. "Where's your dad?"

Between muffled sobs, the girl got out, "Gone."

"Gone where? To a friend's? To town? Where?"

The girl cried a while before she said, "Mom killed him."

"Try not to let it get to you," Courtney said, feeling dumb doing so. "We can't stay put. It's best to move on."

Sniffling and wiping at her nose with her sleeve, the girl drew back. "Leave my home?"

"There might be more of those things," Courtney said. "And with your mom and dad....gone....you can't stay here alone."

"It's our house."

"I know."

"Mom said to never leave it. That we were safe here."

"That didn't work out so hot, did it?"

The girl shook her head, stared at her mother, and began bawling again, her head bowed in misery.

The front door opened and in rushed Billy, holding the shotgun ready to shoot. "Heard a shot," he exclaimed, taking in the situation. "Had to haul Sally with me. Couldn't leave her out there. But she kept dragging her heels."

Behind him, Sally Ann leaned against the jamb, her own face streaked with tears. "I wasn't ready to leave my dad," she said bleakly. "Damn you."

"You can cry your eyes out later," Billy said gruffly. He peered down the hall, then moved to the bottom of the stairs. "Is there anyone else here?"

"The mother and father are dead," Courtney said.

"Brothers? Sisters? We don't want any nasty surprises."

Courtney could have kicked herself for not asking. She bent toward the girl. "Did you hear what he said?"

"There's no one else," the girl replied. "Except Willis."

"Who?"

"Our dog."

Only then did Courtney realize that her own new friend was missing. "Where's Gaga?"

"I didn't see her outside," Billy said. "I thought she was with you."

"God, no," Courtney said, fearing the worst. She tried to remember the last time she saw her. "Gaga!" she yelled. "Where are you?"

From down the hall came a familiar bark.

Followed by a howl that came from something else.

Courtney's fear for Gaga was so strong---so potent---she flew down the hall as if her own life were in peril.

She couldn't say why she liked the dog so much. Gaga was a stray, a mongrel she came across while fleeing zombies in the Twin Cities. They hadn't been together that long. Certainly not long enough to form a deep affection.

Yet there was something about Gaga. The way the dog looked into her eyes. The way Gaga had attached herself to her. The way the dog was always at her side. Until now, anyway.

And after losing her mother and father and sister and brother, Courtney would be damned if she would lose the dog, too.

She raced down the hall, cocking the revolver as she went, and burst into a kitchen prepared to do whatever it took to save her new dog.

Only Gaga didn't need saving.

Over by a table, Gaga was wagging her tail and playfully barking.

On top of the table was a small golden Pomeranian. Crouched low in fear, and quaking, it howled at the ceiling in terror.

Courtney was so relieved, she laughed.

Gaga got her forepaws on a chair and tried to scramble up but lost her footing. The Pomeranian yipped and scooted farther back.

Courtney reached for Gaga's collar just as a small figure dashed past her to the chair. Clambering up, the little girl spread her arms wide and cried, "Willis!" in pure joy.

The Pomeranian ran to her and commenced licking her face in loving abandon.

"So that's your dog," Courtney stated the obvious.

"He's all I have left," the girl said, burying her face in its hair.

"What's your name?" Courtney thought to ask.

"Sansa," the girl said while nuzzling the Pomeranian. "Sansa Kent. My mom named me it because she liked some show on TV." Deep sorrow etched her face and her eyes filled with tears.

"Be strong, Sansa," Courtney said. "We have to get out of here."

"There's no one else here but me," Sansa said. "Now that my mom...." She stopped.

"There was her and the bull and we don't know what else." Courtney paused. "How is it the green cloud didn't do anything to you?"

"Green cloud?" Sansa said. "Oh. That must be when mom put me down in the root cellar. I heard her coughing a lot and when she finally told me to come up, she was changing into...."

"That's all right," Courtney cut her short. "Come on. Let's go." She was eager to get out of there.

"What's your rush?" Billy said from the doorway. "There has to be food in those cupboards and I'm starved."

"Would it be safe to eat? After a green cloud passed through?"

"Food in cans should be." Billy opened a cupboard, and snorted. "Nothing but dishes."

"We don't know what a green cloud can do to stuff in cans," Courtney said. "Do you really want to take the risk?"

"I don't," said a new voice, and Sally Ann entered. She had a strange look about her, a glint to her eyes that Courtney never saw before.

"You're back to yourself?" Billy said. "Good."

"My dad just died, you jackass," Sally Ann said. "Show some feelings, even if you don't have any."

"Hey now," Billy said.

Sally Ann turned to Courtney. "We should get while the getting is good. There will be other farms, other houses. An hour or so down the road, it should be safe to stop and eat."

"You're guessing," Courtney said.

"Hold on," Billy said, going to the table. "Listen, kid...."

"Sansa," Courtney said.

"Listen, Sansa. I'm Billy. We'll take care of you if you want. And you can help us." He gestured. "Are there any guns in the house? Was your dad a hunter or...."

"He had a rifle," Sansa said. "Upstairs in their bedroom."

"Hot damn!" Billy whisked out before anyone could say another word.

"All he thinks about are weapons," Courtney said.

"He's being sensible," Sally Ann said. "If we'd had a rifle, my dad might be alive."

"I'm really sorry....," Courtney began.

"Don't go there,," Sally Ann said coldly. "I've already put him from my mind. He was a jackass and got what was coming to him."

"How can you say that about your own dad?"

"It's a new, vicious, world out there, bestie," Sally Ann said. "Wake up and smell the blood and guts."

CHAPTER 5

Billy was in the lead, the rifle he had found at the farmhouse held firmly in both hands. Around his waist was a cartridge belt with some of the biggest bullets Courtney ever saw. The rifle was something called a Marlin .45-70. Billy seemed to think it could drop just about anything.

She was a few yards behind him, Gaga by her right leg, Sansa on her left. Willis was on a leash, one end wrapped around Sansa's wrist.

Last came Sally Ann. She carried the shotgun and wore the bandolier. On her it looked out of place, as if she were pretending to look tough.

Courtney didn't say so, of course. Her friend was upset enough over her father's death, and acting very unlike herself. As if she were mad at the world and everyone in it.

The farm was half a mile behind them. They were sticking to the road and so far had lucked out. There was no sign of more mutates. No sign of zombies, either. Or anyone else.

"How old are you, Sansa?" Courtney posed a question she realized she should have asked sooner.

"Eight," the girl said. "I'm small for my age. My mom says I take after her mom, who was short her whole life." She stopped, and her lower lip quivered.

Not wanting the girl to burst into tears, Courtney said, "I want you to know something. From here on out, I'll look after you as if you were my own sister." She meant it, which surprised her. Before the bombs and missiles hit, she didn't give a damn about much of anything---or anyone. Her brother annoyed her, her sister was always underfoot, her mom was too bossy, and her dad worked so much, she hardly ever saw him.

"That's awful nice of you. I don't have anyone else." Sansa said. She glanced back and wistfully added, "If you hadn't come along, I might have stayed there forever."

"Weren't you scared? With your mom as she was?"

"She was my mom," Sansa said. "I couldn't leave her. So I hid out up in the attic. I was real careful. She only spotted me once but didn't come after me."

"Didn't she ever leave?" Courtney wondered. It was unlike a mutate to stay in one place. They tended to roam all over in search of prey.

"Hardly ever. Most of the time she sat at the kitchen table."

"She just sat there?" Courtney said in disbelief.

"With her head down. Sometimes she cried. I could hear her from clear upstairs."

"I didn't know mutates could do that."

Behind them Sally Ann chimed in with, "Maybe she didn't turn all the way. Maybe a spark of humanity remained."

They were approaching a bend in the road, framed by woods. Billy wedged his new rifle to his shoulder and slowed.

Courtney put her hand on the revolver. The trees were thick along the road's edge, hiding whatever lay around the bend.

"You hear that?" Sansa said.

A heartbeat later Gaga growled.

"Hold up!" Courtney said quietly to Billy.

"What for?" Billy said. But he stopped.

Courtney strained her ears. Faintly, she heard a peculiar sort of grunting and scraping. "Stay here," she whispered to Sansa. Hurrying past Billy, she said, "You too. I want to take a look."

"Better if it's the both of us," Billy said.

"Stay with the girl."

"Well, hell, Courts...."

Courtney wasn't listening. To him. She was trying to make sense of what she was hearing from up ahead. Crouching, she edged forward until she could see the next stretch of road.

The first thing that hit her was the stench of gasoline.

Two vehicles had collided. A large farm tractor and a tanker truck. The best Courtney could guess, the tractor---a green John Deere--- had either been in the middle of the road or trying to cross when the tanker came barreling around the bend and slammed into it. The impact had crumpled the tractor like so much tin foil and sent it skidding on its side into a field. As for the tanker, it was on its side, too, blocking the road, the red semi canted at an angle, the white tank ruptured near the top. Gas had spilled out, gallons and gallons, forming a gas pond around the truck that had since dried. But the stink remained.

Straightening, Courtney ventured around the bend. The scraping grew louder, and she saw that the truck driver was still in the cab. The crash had killed him, and now, in typical zombie fashion, he was scraping at a window in a vain effort to be free.

Courtney figured the farmer in the tractor must be

dead too. Then something tugged at her leg.

Courtney screamed. She didn't mean to. It tore out of her even as she kicked and sprang back, half startled out of her wits.

The farmer from the tractor---or what was left of him---was on the ground at her feet. How she hadn't noticed him, she couldn't say. She'd almost stepped on him.

It was well she hadn't.

From the waist up he was a big, burly man, with a rugged face and a square jaw. Now most of his left shoulder and left arm were gone, his face was a gashed ruin, and his jaw looked as if it had been split by a hatchet. From the waist down there was nothing; he had somehow been split in half. Intestines dragged on the ground in his wake as he grunted and clawed anew at her leg.

Courtney skipped back, drawing the Vaquero. She wasn't quite fast enough. The farmer's big hand closed on her foot. She tried to jerk loose but suddenly her leg was yanked out from under her, and the next she knew, she was on her side in the road, her back to the zombie, and her revolver spun loose from her grasp.

Wincing at the pain, she rose on an elbow and looked over her shoulder. Straight into the zombie's eyes. Eyes that were glazed and lifeless yet lit by a craving from beyond the grave.

"No!" Courtney cried, and tried to scramble away. Fingers as hard as iron and as cold as ice clamped onto her shoulder.

The farmer's mouth gaped, and he bit at her neck.

In utter terror, Courtney broke free and scrabbled toward the gun. The zombie slithered after her. That it only had one arm slowed it but not as much as she would have expected. Her hand was inches from the revolver when the zombie's hand latched onto her hair.

Courtney cried out as her head was yanked back so hard, it was a wonder her spine didn't snap. She punched the thing's arm but it didn't seem to feel her blows. Again her head was yanked, and now she found herself on her back with the zombie seeking to slide on top of her.

Courtney pushed but the thing clung fast. Its hand shifted from her hair to her neck. She felt its nails dig into her flesh, felt the wetness of blood. She bucked upward but all that did was bring its face closer to hers.

In her mind's eye she saw the zombie sink its teeth into her cheek. Saw it tear her cheek half off and gulp the morsel like a seal gulping a fish.

Then a shot boomed and the top of the zombie's head burst. Gore and bits spatterd her, and she whipped her head to one side to keep the stuff from getting into her mouth and nose and eyes.

The zombie sagged, motionless, and at last Courtney was able to heave it off. Sitting up, she grabbed the revolver, pushed to her feet, and took aim.

"A little late for that," Billy said. He was ten feet away, the .45-70 to his shoulder.

Sansa ran up and wrapped her arms around Courtney's leg. "I was so scared for you!" she exclaimed.

Sally Ann stepped to the zombie and poked it with a toe. "Stupid," she said.

"Their brains don't work," Courtney said. "You know that."

"I meant you," Sally Ann said, shaking her head. "Letting it catch you like that. It doesn't even have legs."

"I didn't see it."

"Situational awareness," Sally Ann said. "Never leave home without it these days."

"What's gotten into you?" Courtney said. "You used to be more considerate."

"Ladies," Billy said. "Gripe later. That shot might brings others. We should make ourselves scarce." He limped on, moving off the road to avoid the truck.

Sansa tugged on Willis's leash and followed.

Gaga, to Courtney great surprise, went with them.

"Your mutt has a new friend," Sally Ann said.

"Cut it out," Courtney said.

"We need to talk anyway," Sally Ann said. "Just the two of us.'

They walked together, neither saying anything until they were past the tanker.

"All right. Listen up," Sally Ann began. "We've been friends since elementary school, right?"

"Yeah, so?"

"So don't go off on me when I tell you that you have to get your act together."

"Excuse me?"

"Don't play dumb," Sally Ann said. "That thing should never have gotten close to you. Yet it almost did you in."

"It snuck up on me," Courtney said.

Sally Ann said and sighed. "You have to up your game, girlfriend. I mean it. If you don't, you'll never reach that compound we're hoping to find. Toughen up. Or else."

CHAPTER 6

Courtney hated being lectured. Her mom used to do it and usually Courtney just shut her out and then went and did as she wanted to anyway. Her dad didn't lecture so much. When she broke their rules, he punished her. Grounding, usually. Although now and then he took her phone.

But to have her best friend act like her mom rankled. Especially since Sally Ann wasn't the bossy type. Sally was smart, and knew things a lot of people didn't. But she didn't flaunt it. She wasn't one of those know-it-all's.

It didn't help Courtney's mood any that Sally Ann walked ahead to be with Billy instead of her.

At least Courtney had Gaga. She patted Gaga on the head and received a warm lick in return.

"You and me against the world," Courtney said.

"Me too," Sansa said. "I like how you talk to your dog. I talk to Willis all the time."

"Does he ever answer?" Courtney joked.

"He's a dog," Sansa said, as if it were the dumbest question in the world. "Dogs can't talk."

"Just not my day," Courtney said.

"Pardon."

"Nothing." Courtney wanted to keep talking so she said, "From here on out, I want you to stick close to me. We never know when something might happen."

"Something bad you mean," Sansa said. She

scrunched her face in thought, then said, "Why do bad things happen, anyway?"

"You're asking me?"

"Yes."

"Girl, how would I know?" Courtney said. "We're born into this world with no say over how things are. If we're lucky, we get through life without a lot of bad things happening. If not..." She shrugged.

"This is bad," Sansa said, motioning at the world around them.

"It's become so, yes."

Sansa looked at her. "Does God really love us, like my mom used to say? If so, how could all of this happen?"

"Damn, you ask hard questions," Courtney said without thinking. She frowned. "I don't have the answers, kiddo. To anything. I've always sort of tried to make it through each day one day at a time, you know?"

"No."

"What I'm saying is, you should ask a minister or somebody."

"But what do *you* think? Does God loves us or not?"

"If He does, He has a strange way of showing it."

Sansa laughed.

"You find that funny?"

Sansa gazed into the woods to their right and went to say something, and stopped, her eyes widening.

Courtney spun, Her hand dropped to the revolver but the woods were still. "What did you see?"

"Something...," Sansa said. "I'm not sure."

Courtney probed the shadows for movement. "Describe it?"

"I can't," Sansa said. "It was there and then it wasn't."

"A person?"

"I don't know."

"An animal?"

"I don't know."

Courtney peered deeper into the woods. "A zombie, maybe?"

"Aren't you listening to me?" Sansa said in annoyance. "I didn't get a good look."

"Keep your eyes peeled," Courtney said. "Whatever it is might be stalking us."

They hiked on, Courtney wished their dogs were of more use. Gaga and Willis were only interested in each other. They paid no attention to their surroundings. "Dummies," she said under her breath.

A hill loomed. Billy and Sally Ann reached the crest and stopped.

Sansa was puffing when Courtney and her joined them.

"We resting a bit?" Courtney said.

Billy pointed.

The road ahead was blocked. About fifty yards from the bottom of the hill, a barrier had been erected; two old cars to either side, with a bunch of furniture piled in the middle.

Farther on, a quarter-mile or so, was a cluster of buildings. Lights glowed here and there.

"A town," Billy said.

"A hamlet, more like," Sally Ann said.

"What's the difference?" Billy said.

"Hamlets are smaller. Fewer people."

"Well, whatever, they must have a generator," Billy said. "And they're country folk. They'll be friendly."

"We don't know that," Sally Ann said. "We should

go around."

"Come on, Sal," Billy said. "They might have food they'll share. They might even put us up for the night. Maybe we might get to sleep in a bed for a change."

"Might, might, might," Sally Ann said.

"I vote we go see," Billy said. "You vote we don't." He turned. "That leaves it up to you, Courts. Do we pay them a visit or not?"

Courtney was all for a hot meal and a bed but she remembered Sally Ann's little lecture. "I pass. I don't want to vote."

"Not an option," Sally Ann said. "We're in this together."

Sansa tugged on Courtney's leg. "That's Marysville. My mom and dad took me there now and then. To buy stuff. There's a store. The people were nice."

"You hear that?" Billy gloated.

Courtney made up her mind. "In that case, I vote we go on in."

"God help us if you're wrong," Sally Ann said.

CHAPTER 7

"Get behind me," Billy said as they neared the barricade. He was holding his rifle ready to shoot.

Sally Ann moved up beside him. "We don't need protecting."

Courtney did the same, saying to Sansa, "Hang back with the dogs."

There was no hint of movement and no one challenged them.

Courtney was beginning to think the barricade was untended when a man called out.

"That's far enough, you kids! Stop right there!"

"Who is he calling a kid?" Billy said.

"Grow up," Sally Ann said to him. Holding the shotgun out from her side, she took a couple of steps. "We're friendly, mister! We're just looking for a place to stop and rest."

"Tell the boy to sling his rifle," the man said.

Courtney pinpointed the voice as coming from behind the pile of furniture.

"I'm not no boy!" Billy angrily responded, but he did as the man wanted.

"What's your name?" the man asked.

Billy told him.

"I'm Harry," the man said. "Didn't mean to offend you. It's just we can't take unnecessary risks. We have our families to protect."

"We?" Sally Ann said.

Part of the middle section moved, and Courtney saw that the furniture had been cleverly linked together so it could be slid aside. Two men came through. At the same time, two others came around the cars on the right and the left. All were armed with rifles but they didn't point their weapons.

The stockiest of them was clad in an old denim jacket and dungarees. "I'm Harry Comstock." He was in his forties or so. It was obvious he hadn't been sleeping well. His face was drawn and tired. But he smiled. "Who's the little one?"

"Sansa Kent," Courtney said, and introduced herself, and then Billy and Sally Ann.

Harry was most interested in Sansa. "Did you say Kent? I know a family by that name. A farmer and his wife who live down the road a piece...."

"That's the one," Courtney said.

"Where are her folks?" Harry asked.

Courtney shook her head.

"Damn," Harry said, then coughed. "You're welcome in Marysville. You have to hand over your weapons, though. And you don't go anywhere unescorted."

"My rifle stays with me," Billy declared.

"Be reasonable, son," Harry said. "We can't have armed strangers wandering around. Not with our wives and children. We'll give your weapons back when you want to leave."

"It's the only way you get in," another man said.

"We don't know you from Adam," a third man said. "You can't expect us to trust you right off the bat."

Billy bristled, and Courtney moved past him before his temper got the better of him. "That works both ways, mister. How can we trust you when you don't trust us?"

"Oh, for crying out loud," Sally Ann said. Marching up to Harry, she handed him her shotgun, then turned. "They don't trust us. We don't trust them. Fine. But this man knew Sansa's parents...."

"Not well," Harry said. "I run a service station, and they'd stop for gas."

"You see?" Sally Ann said. "How more honest could he be." She gestured. "Go around Marysville if you two want. But I'm going in. I want some hot food and a good night's rest and I really don't think they're going to slit our throats in the middle of the night."

"Good God, girl," said a thin man over by a car. "What do you take us for?"

Sally Ann went on through.

Courtney drew her revolver and held it out. "It's been rough for us."

"Ms. Hewitt, wasn't it?" Harry said. "It's been rough for all of us." He accepted the revolver.

Courtney took Sansa's hand. Together they walked through the gap , Gaga and Willis trailing along.

Courtney stopped and looked back. "Billy? We've come this far. We shouldn't separate."

"I'm doing this for you," Billy said. He thrust his rifle at Harry.

Sally Ann had waited for them. "Lighten up, will you?"

"I can't help it," Billy said. "We've nearly been killed how many times now?"

Sally Ann smiled at the lights in the distance. "I have a good feeling about this. Maybe if they like us they'll let us stay."

"What about the compound we heard about on the

radio?" Courtney said.

"It's way up north," Sally Ann reminded her. "Why go that far if we don't have to? Let's enjoy ourselves. It could be the worst is behind us."

"You hope," Billy said.

Harry Comstock and the tall man escorted them into Marysville.

Courtney didn't know what she was expecting but it certainly wasn't how normal everything appeared.

The hamlet consisted of about a dozen houses and two places of business. Harry's gas station sat at the junction of the main road with a side street. Across from it was a small market. Both were open.

Night was hours off, yet thanks to the overcast sky, it was so dark, the street lights had come on and the market and the gas station were well lit.

"Generators," Harry explained when Sally Ann asked how that was possible. "The winters here, as you probably know, are pretty fierce. Cold as can be, and a lot of snow. We have the generators for when the power goes out."

"How long will it be before you run out of fuel?" Sally Ann asked.

"Months," Harry said. "We'll find more before we do."

Not a lot of people were out and about.

Courtney wondered why aloud, and Harry told her that most were home doing what they would normally be doing.

"Mothers are taking care of their kids. The dads, most of them, are at the barricades to the north and south."

"What about the east and west?" Sally Ann said.

Harry idly waved a hand at the open fields that stretched for a mile or more in either direction. "As you can see, nothing can get at us either side without us spotting it from a long ways off."

"And the zombies?" Sally Ann said.

Harry shrugged. "We haven't seen that many. The few we have, we picked off easy enough."

"You've been lucky, mister," Billy remarked. "There are thousands of the things in the Twin Cities."

"We're a long ways from Minneapolis and St. Paul," Harry said. "Why would they come out this far?"

"Food," Billy said. "Fresh meat to munch on."

Harry and the tall man exchanged looks of annoyance. "I'll thank you not to bring that up while you're staying here. We don't want to needlessly scare our families."

"You ask me, Mr. Comstock," Sally Ann said, "you're in denial."

By then they were at the market.

"Let's go in," Billy said eagerly. "I want to buy a six-pack and enough food to fill my backpack."

"I'm afraid not," Harry said.

"How come?" Billy said.

"Nothing is for sale," Harry said. "Not here, nor the gas station. We're saving what we have for us." He held up a hand when Billy went to speak. "That doesn't mean we won't share. The four of you are welcome to spend the night at the Jasper place. Their cupboards are full of canned goods."

"They won't mind putting us up?" Courtney said.

"They're not to home," Harry said. "They took off for the Twin Cities the day before the war broke out to put Mrs. Jasper's mother in a nursing home. She has dementia." Harry scowled. "They haven't come back. So you can have the run of their house," Harry continued. "Eat their food. Sleep in their beds. In the morning we'll have a talk about whether you move on or stay." He clapped Billy on the shoulder. "We could use another man to help out with guard duties and whatnot."

"Hey, Courts and I can do our share," Sally Ann said. "We've killed zombies."

"Aren't you the toughie," Harry joked, but no one laughed. "Come on. I'll show you where the Jaspers live."

It was down the side street about a block, on the left, a two-story frame house with a peaked roof and a front porch.

Harry opened the front door and walked on in. The curtains were open, admitting enough light to reveal a comfortably furnished living room with a huge sofa.

"There are candles in a kitchen drawer," Harry informed them. "The stove is gas, hooked to a tank out back. I ask that you keep everything as neat as you find it, and that you don't let your dogs do their business inside."

"You have our word," Sally Ann said.

"All right, then." Harry paused at the door and indicated the tall man, who was on the porch. "Chester will be across the street. You need anything, give him a holler."

"Across the street keeping an eye on us," Sally Ann said.

Harry smiled and winked and left, closing the door behind him.

"I wish they'd given our guns back," Billy said.

"Chill, will you?" Sally Ann said. "Let's get some candles lit and see what there is to eat and settle in. We're safe here, people."

Courtney wanted to believe her. But a tiny voice deep inside warned her not to.

CHAPTER 8

The evening passed wonderfully. Billy surprised them by announcing that he would cook. Courtney suspected it had to do with the giant can of beef stew he found in a cupboard. A loaf of bread, and butter from the fridge, provided them with a veritable feast.

Courtney never liked canned food all that much but the stew was delicious.

Everyone was in good spirits until Sansa started to talk about the green cloud that passed over the Kent farm. Sally Ann cut her off and brought up that they should turn in early to be well rested for tomorrow.

Truth to tell, Courtney was beat. The meal, the warmth, had made her drowsy.

There were only two bedrooms. Sally Ann suggested they draw lots to see who would sleep on the sofa. Billy volunteered, saying it wasn't fair that 'you lovely ladies' should have to.

Sansa cleared her throat. "I want to sleep on the sofa, if it's okay."

"Why?" Courtney wanted to know.

"Upstairs will make me think of home, and my mom," Sansa said glumly.

"The sofa it is, then," Courtney said. "Provided you don't mind company. It's big enough for two, and we can keep an eye on our dogs."

Courtney and Sansa took Willis and Gaga out to do their business before turning in. The other houses along the side street all had lit windows. Smoke curled from chimneys. Out on the road, the street lights cast circles of light. Somewhere, music played.

"It sure is nice here," Sansa said.

Courtney was noting how the clouds had a strange glow about them, and how the wind whispered as if it were a multitude of voices. Involuntarily, she shivered.

"You okay, Courts?" Sansa asked. She had taken to calling her by Billy's pet name.

"Why wouldn't I be?" Courtney said. She saw a lanky figure by the house across the street, who she took to be Chester.

"Do you want to stay here like Sally does?" Sansa asked.

"I haven't made up my mind yet."

They went back inside.

The dogs, exhausted, sprawled on a rug.

Sally Ann brought down folded blankets and said she was turning in. Billy already had.

"How about we each take an end?" Courtney suggested. The sofa was big enough that they could curl up with plenty of room.

Yawning, Sansa was barely able to keep her eyes open as Courtney tucked her in.

"Thank you for looking after me," the girl said, her eyelids drooping.

"No problem."

Courtney moved to her end, adjusted the pillow, lay on her side, and covered herself with the blanket. Warmth spread through her, and she felt herself relax. That tiny voice flared to life, warning her to stay alert, but her fatigue was a black cloak enfolding her mind. She drifted into a vast stillness.

Then, suddenly, she was wide awake.

Courtney realized she had rolled over while she slept and was now facing the back of the sofa. Her cheek was on the pillow. The blanket had slipped partway off, and she was chilly. She pulled the blanket higher and snuggled in again. This was her best sleep in days.

She could hear Sansa breathing, hear Willis snore. Small as he was, from his snores you'd think he was a Great Dane.

Courtney smiled. She was on the verge of sleep when a new sound registered. A sound as if something were brushing against the house. A tree limb, she reckoned, blown by the wind. But she didn't hear the wind, and she didn't recall seeing a tree anywhere near the house.

The brushing sound stopped.

Courtney slid farther under the blanket. She was worrying over nothing. She emptied her head and lethargy crept through her and just when she was about to go out like a light, suddenly she was awake once more.

She needed to get a grip. Her nerves were so frayed, they were spoiling her rest. She lay quiet, hoping to drift off again. She listened to Sansa breathe and Willis snore, and grinned. All was well.

No sooner did she tell herself that than new sounds intruded. This time there was no mistaking them for the wind. There was no mistaking them for anything other than what they were.

Footsteps.

On the front porch.

Courtney slid her head out from under the blanket and rolled over.

The footsteps faded away.

She wondered if it had been the tall guy who was keeping an eye on them. Or maybe some other Marysville resident. But why would someone be checking on them in the middle of the night?

Courtney waited, and when she didn't hear any new sounds, she pulled the blanket up again and closed her eyes. At last she could enjoy a few more hours undisturbed slumber.

The footsteps returned.

Along with other vague noises.

Anger compelled Courtney to get up. Wrapping the blanket around her, she moved to the door and pressed an ear to the wood. Just as she did, there was a scratching noise on the other side, causing her to jump back.

A sense of unease came over her. She glanced at the window. Even though it was dark out, shadows appeared to be playing across the glass between the open curtains.

Slowly sidling over, careful not to show herself, Courtney peeked past the near curtain. Her breath caught in her throat and she shivered, but not from the chill.

The porch crawled with zombies. Or, rather, they were shambling across it in a steady stream from left to right, some dragging one leg or the other.

The number staggered her. Dozens went by and yet more came after them. Out past the porch, more figures shuffled and lurched.

It wasn't a stream.

It was a river.

Courtney drew back before one of them spotted her. Her brain was alive with questions. How could there be so many? Where did they all come from? They couldn't have approached the hamlet from up or down the road or the sentries at the barricades would have given the alarm. No, the creatures must be pouring out of the woods to the east. A swarm from the Twin Cities, possibly. Sally Ann had been saying that once the zombies in the cities finished off the people there, they would spread to the countryside.

Over on the sofa, Sansa mumbled and rolled over.

Willis stopped snoring.

Gaga sat up.

The last thing Courtney needed was for either dog to bark and give them away. Sliding her hand behind the curtain, she groped and found the cord to the traverse rod. She slowly pulled it to close the curtains but no sooner did she start then there was a thunk against the glass.

A face was pressed against the pane. A ghastly face, the eyes glazed, half of a cheek gone, the lower lip dangling.

Courtney stopped pulling.

The zombie seemed to be trying to press its face through the glass. Why, Courtney had no idea. She saw its tongue move, saw slobber or drool trickle down. The thing was licking the window!

Gaga growled, softly.

"Quiet," Courtney whispered.

Sansa did more mumbling and rolling.

There was another scratch on the front door.

Courtney had left her revolver on the floor next to the sofa. She could reach it in several quick steps, and tensed to do just that.

With a slight sucking sound, the creature at the

window drew back, stiffly turned, and rejoined the flow of living dead.

Dreading another zombie would notice, Courtney closed the curtains. She moved to the stairs to go up and wake Sally Ann and Billy but someone was coming down.

"We're in trouble," Sally Ann whispered.

"Don't I know it," Courtney said.

"You saw them too?" Sally Ann said. "Something woke me, and I looked out the upstairs window. I can't believe how many there are."

"Hundreds," Courtney said.

"Thousands," Sally Ann said.

"What do we do?" It dawned on Courtney that she was relying more and more on her friend's judgement of late.

"Nothing."

"Be serious."

"I am," Sally Ann said. "The things were probably drawn by the streetlights. If they don't see anyone, if the sentries and the people in the houses are smart enough to lie low, the zombies might pass on through without attacking anybody."

"I don't like being hemmed in," Courtney said.

"What choice do we have?" Sally Ann whispered. "There are too many for us to try and break out."

"Just when I thought things were going great for once," Courtney said.

"We're alive, aren't we?" Sally Ann said. "Just keep your fingers crossed."

That was when a scream knifed the night.

CHAPTER 9

It came from close by, a keening cry of utter terror. A cry that tore at the heart. A cry the likes of which that those who heard it would never forget it.

Sansa jerked up on the sofa and uttered a cry of her own.

Quickly, Courtney moved to the girl and put an arm around her to comfort her---and to keep her from cyring out a second time. "It's all right. I'm right here."

"We need to stay quiet," Sally Ann whispered.

Willis had scrambled up and now was looking all around in confusion. Tilting his head, he sniffed, and let out a snarl worthy of a wolf.

"Shhh!" Courtney said, reaching for him.

The little dog sprang toward the door, growling deep in his throat.

Sally Ann tried to grab him but he scooted past and commenced to scratch at the front door, and snarl.

"The zombies!" Sally Ann said, and scooped him up.

Feet pounded on the stairs and down into the living room rushed Billy. "What the hell?" he exclaimed. "Some noise woke me. What's going on?"

"Keep it down, will you?" Courtney cautioned. "There are zombies all over."

"What?" Billy said. He stepped to the curtains and reached out.

"Don't!" Courtney exclaimed.

Billy yanked.

Half a dozen dead faces peered in at them, some with their mouths working as if eager to chew flesh, some with their clawed fingers on the glass.

Quickly closing the curtain, Billy turned, his shock evident. "What in the world has happened?"

"Isn't it obvious?" Sally Ann said. "Marysville is being overrun."

As if to confirm her assessment, a second scream, and yet a third, pierced the night air, followed by the boom of gunshots.

Billy moved to the door. "We have to help them!"

"No!" Sally Ann said. Dropping Willis, she lunged and grabbed Billy's arm. "Are you insane? You wouldn't last a minute out there!"

More gunshots and more screams added to the rising bedlam. Somewhere glass broke with a ringing crash. A dog howled in pain.

Courtney felt Sansa tremble.

The scratching on the door and the window grew louder.

"They were nice to us, they let us stay here," Billy said, but not loudly. "I don't like doing nothing."

Sally Ann stared at the ceiling. "Is there an attic in this place? A cellar? Somewhere we can hole up? I didn't think to look."

"Me either," Billy said. "I'll go through the house and..."

"No," Courtney said. "We stick together." She pulled Sansa to her feet and retrieved the revolver.

A fist struck the door, shaking it.

"Stay close." Holding onto Sansa's hand, with Willis following, Courtney headed down the hall. She preferred a basement over an attic. There were likely to be windows they could escape through if the creatures broke in. Sure, an attic might have windows, but they would have to drop two stories.

Courtney was halfway to the kitchen when there was a loud cracking sound and the back door was flung wide. She didn't wait to see what came through. On her left was an open doorway and she darted in, hoping the others would have the presence of mind to follow suit.

It was a laundry room, barely big enough for all of them to squeeze into. A washer and drier were against one side, a shelf with detergent and other stuff on the opposite wall. A small window was high on the wall across from the door.

Gaga pressed against Courtney's leg as she made room for the others.

Billy was last in. He shut the door and put his shoulder to it, listening.

They all heard the shuffling of feet.

Billy raised a finger to his lips.

From the front of the house came a crash.

Setting Sansa down, Courtney whispered in her ear, "Be very still." She reached up and gripped the bottom of the window sill. It took considerable effort to pull herself high enough to see out.

The window hadn't been cleaned in ages. Hooking an elbow on the sill, Courtney swiped at the dust with her fingertips. Grass blocked most of her view.

"Any zombies?" Sally Ann said.

"Can't tell."

"Here," Sally Ann said, snatching a washcloth off a shelf. "Try this."

Courtney let herself down, took the cloth. Braced on her forearm, she rubbed the cloth back and forth.

The best she could tell, the window faced a side yard. There was the outline of a fence.

"Well?" Sally Ann said.

"I don't see any."

"Then out you go," Sally Ann said. "I'll boost you so you can open the window."

"Maybe we should wait," Billy whispered. "The things in the house might wander off."

As if to prove him wrong, the laundry room door shook to a powerful blow.

Courtney half expected Sansa to cry out or recoil in fear but the little one surprised her.

Sansa glared at the door and said as calmly as could be, "We have to get out of here."

Sally Ann took a position below the window and cupped her hands. "Hurry!"

Courtney hooked her foot in her friend's palms and was levered high enough to work the latch. She twisted but it wouldn't turn. It hadn't been used in so long, it was stuck.

Another blow shook the door.

"Make it fast, Courts," Billy said, leveling the rifle.

Courtney twisted so hard, her fingers hurt. Just when she thought she might have to break the glass, the latch gave. She pulled upward but the window wouldn't budge. Using both hands, she tugged with all her might, and nearly lost her balance.

"Careful," Sally Ann said. "Almost dropped you."

"Open, damn you!" Courtney said under her breath, and tugged until her arms hurt. With loud creaks, the hinges loosened and the window swung open.

Courtney cautiously stuck her head out. They were in luck. The window opened onto a small fenced area where the family kept their trash and recycle bin. The fence was five feet high, with a gate that was closed.

"What are you waiting for?" Sally Ann whispered.

Courtney slid her shoulders through. It was a tight fit but by wriggling and squirming she made it out. Shoving her hand down, she said, "Sansa next."

"No. Do Willis," the girl said. She was clasping the dog to her as if for dear life.

"You," Courtney said, "and don't argue. Then the dogs."

The door was shaken by the most violent blow yet.

"God, will you get your tails in gear?" Billy said. "This won't hold forever."

Sally Ann lifted Sansa high enough that Courtney could slip her hands under the girl's arms and pull her through. Sansa had the presence of mind to hold herself perfectly still. Once out, she crouched and tried to peer past Courtney.

"Willis!" she said softly. "Please!"

Thankfully, the little dog didn't struggle. But when it was Gaga's turn, she whined and tried to pull away.

Courtney felt her grip slipping. "Help me, Sal!"

Between them, they got Gaga out.

Sally Ann handed the shotgun up, then jumped and caught hold of the ledge.

Courtney seized her forearms and braced herself as Sally Ann used her elbows and knees to best advantage. Sally's shoulders were wider than hers, and it was tight fit, but together they managed it.

"Damn, that hurt," Sally Ann complained, rubbing her arms.

Courtney was thinking of Billy. She thrust her hand down but he was still over by the door. "What are you waiting for?"

Blows were raining on the door nonstop.

Billy raised his rifle as if to shoot.

"For God's sake, no!" Courtney whispered "It will only excite them and draw more."

Reluctantly, Billy lowered the .45-70 and came to the window. "Take it," he said, holding the rifle up.

Courtney passed it to Sally Ann, then lowered her arms as far as they would go.

"Back away," Billy said. "I can do it myself."

Courtney didn't argue. The door was shaking so violently, it wouldn't last much longer.

For an athlete like Billy, it was simple to leap and shove his arms out and get hold of either side of the frame. His head and neck came out easy. But when he tried to shove his shoulders through, they came partway, and stuck.

The door was quaking like a leaf in a gale.

Billy thrashed furiously. He strained until his neck muscles bulged and he was red in the face. And was still stuck.

"If it's not one thing....," Billy muttered, and wriggled furiously, flapping his legs to try and gain momentum.

A crack appeared in the door. Not a large one, but part of a ghastly face was visible.

Billy swore and kicked and still couldn't make it out.

"Let me help," Courtney said. Grabbing his hands, she dug in her heels and heaved backward. Billy grimaced in pain but didn't cry out. The edges of the metal jambs were digging into him, tearing his shirt and the skin underneath. Courtney heaved again and once once more, pulling him a few more inches. Blood appeared on his shirt.

Courtney took a deep breath and bunched her body....and the top of the door crashed inward.

CHAPTER 10

Courtney envisioned zombies pouring into the laundry room and biting and ripping at Billy's legs but so many zombies tried to force themselves through the opening that they became entangled and not one made it through.

Sally Ann took hold of Billy's right arm. "You take his left. On the count of three."

"Hurry, ladies!" Billy grit his teeth. His shirt was ,becoming more red by the moment.

Sally Ann counted.

At "Three!", Courtney and her threw themselves backward, their legs taut, their arms like iron bars.

Billy gasped, blood dripping from each shoulder. Suddenly they were through.

Courtney and Sally Ann pulled until he was all the way out. When they let go, he clutched his arms and doubled over.

"Everyone down!" Courtney said, and turning to Sansa, who was holding Willis, pulled the girl flat on the grass.

With a rending crash, the door fell to the floor and zombies burst into the laundry room. Teeth chomped. Glazed eyes rolled about. They turned this way and that. Several reached toward the window, but seeing it was empty, they lost interest and milled with the rest.

Their confusion was almost comical.

Sliding backward until she was sure she couldn't be

seen, Courtney rose into a crouch and sat with her back to the fence.

Sansa clung to her arm. Gaga's nose was against her leg.

Sally Ann joined them, and grinned and whispered, "Whew! That was close!"

Billy was curled on his side near the window, his hands over the gashes in his arms. He went to say something but Courtney put a finger to her lips.

Slowing rising, she peered over the fence. To her surprise, the only zombies she saw were a few out toward the street.

Sinking down, Courtney wearily leaned back. The night had gone strangely quiet. "We're safe for a bit," she whispered.

Sally Ann sat against the fence, too. Rubbing her shoulder, she said, "You sure are heavy, Billy. I thought my arm was going to pop out of its socket."

"It's all that muscle," Courtney said.

With a grunt, Billy sat up and came over, "Didn't ever think you'd noticed." He gingerly pried at the rips in his right sleeve. "Damn, this hurts."

"Let me have a look," Courtney said.

"I'm all right."

Swatting his hand aside, Courtney examined him. Both of his upper arms were torn and bleeding. But the blood flow was stopping. He'd have nasty gashes that would take a while to heal but he would be good as new eventually.

"First my leg and now this," Billy said.

"Think of the millions who have died so far," Sally Ann said. "Compared to them, we're having it easy."

"Doesn't feel easy," Billy said.

"We should bandage you up," Courtney suggested. "To prevent infection."

"Bandage me with what?" Billy said. "We're not going back in that house."

"We'll find something....," Courtney began.

A scream rent the darkness. This time it was torn from the throat of a man. It rose to a piercing shriek and ended in a drawn-out gurgle.

"Someone from Marysville," Sally Ann said in horror.

"Wonder how many are left?" Billy said.

As in answer, the night erupted in gunfire and shouts.

Courtney pushed to her feet. "That's coming from the gas station and the store."

"There must be people holed up in them," Sally Ann said.

"We should help," Billy said, reaching for his rifle.

"As many zombies as are out there, we wouldn't last ten minutes," Courtney said.

More shots cracked. From the difference in the sounds, Courtney judged there were three or four people firing at once.

"The shots will draw those things aways from us," Sally Ann said. "We should get while the getting is good."

"And just leave Harry and them?" Billy said.

"For all we know, he's already dead," Sally Ann said. She moved toward the gate. "Get your butts in gear. We're out of here."

"Sal, wait," Courtney said.

"We're leaving. Now!" Sally Ann opened the gate...and there, hunched over, was a man.

It wasn't just any man. It was the tall one who had

escorted them to the house, the man Courtney last saw across the street. He was stooped down, bent double, his arms wrapped around his belly, vomit on the ground in front of him, more vomit spilling over his lower lip.

As the gate opened, he looked up. He wore the most pained expression. His eyes and Courtney's met, and even in the dark she could tell his were brown, and he was still human. But that very instant his eyes paled and glazed and just-like-that he wasn't human anymore.

Courtney was at a loss as to how he got there. Maybe he had tried to reach them when the swarm first appeared. Maybe one had bitten him and he only now turned.

Snarling he clawed for Sally Ann, who was riveted in surprise.

The thunder of Billy's .45-70 was abominably loud in the enclosed space. At the blast, the top of the man's head exploded and he fell.

The shot would bring more creatures, as sure as anything.

"Run!" Courtney cried to all of the others. "Run for your lives!"

Courtney grabbed Sansa's hand and told her to hold tight to Willis. She was out the gate a few steps ahead of Sally Ann. Billy came last, limping. His leg was bothering him again.

At the front corner of the house Courtney stopped to get her bearings and assess the situation.

No zombies were in their immediate vicinity. The gas station and store were surrounded, the horde bathed in the garish light of the street lamps. The zombies were striking the store fronts, trying to get in.

There was nothing Courtney or anyone could do to

help whoever was trapped inside. There were simply too many of the ravenous dead.

From across the street came the sound of something being smashed. A zombie shuffled out the front door of a house. Another was coming around the side.

Others were coming from the main road, to their right.

Courtney turned left and broke into a jog. She couldn't go as fast as she would like because of Sansa. Gaga easily kept pace but the girl had to take two steps for each of hers.

They passed the front door. It hung by a single hinge, and zombies were shambling across the living room to reach it.

Courtney tore her gaze from them....and almost collided with another that loomed out of the night. A skinny man, his clothes in tatters, his flesh torn to ribbons, his face worse than Frankenstein's.

Without thinking, Courtney pulled her revolver and shot him in the head.

"Now they'll be all over us!" Sally Ann exclaimed.

"Couldn't be helped," Courtney said, and ran, hauling Sansa with her.

Sticking to the grass, to the yards, where the shadows were deeper, they passed a second house, and a third. The block ended abruptly at the edge of woodland.

Once in there, they could lose the creatures. Or so Courtney hoped.

"Look out!" Billy yelled.

A fast zombie was running toward them. Rarer than the slow kind, the fast ones could move as quickly as a normal person.

This one hurtled at Courtney with its mouth agape

and its fingers splayed. She tried to point the Vaquero but the thing was on her before she could shoot. A forearm swatted the barrel aside. Its other hand caught in her hair even as it rammed a shoulder into her chest and sent her stumbling.

Panicked, Courtney struck at its face. She tripped, attempted to keep her balance, and felt one of the zombie's leg catch behind hers. She fell flat on her back. A knee caught her in the gut. The creature snapped at her arm, but missed.

Then Gaga sprang, tearing at the thing's chest. It ignored the dog.

Courtney slammed her revolver against its cheek and nearly had her hand bit.

Raw fear spiked through her. Not for herself. For little Sansa, who threw herself at the thing and started punching it.

"Leave Courts be!" Sansa cried.

The creature backhanded her and sent the girl flying.

It knocked Gaga aside, too.

It was only interested in Courtney. Only interested in sinking its slavering mouth into her flesh.

Courtney heaved but couldn't cast the thing off. Was it her imagination, or did those glazed eyes light with an inner fire as it swooped at her throat?

CHAPTER 11

"Eat this!"

Courtney shoved the Vaquero's barrel into the thing's gaping mouth. The hammer was already back so all she had to do was squeeze the trigger.

The head burst, spewing bone and hair and brains every which way. The creature collapsed, its face within an inch of Courtney's.

Hands reached down, and Billy flung the zombie off. "You all right? Were you bit?"

"Don't think so," Courtney said, struggling to collect her wits.

"I tried to shoot but didn't have a clear shot," Billy said. "I was afraid I'd hit you."

"Same here," Sally Ann said.

Courtney made it to her knees and Billy helped her the rest of the way. When he stepped back, Sansa ran up and embraced her legs.

"I was so scared for you!"

"Makes two of us," Billy said.

"People," Sally Ann said, glancing about. "This is touching and all---but we have to haul butt. Now!"

More zombies---the slow variety---were approaching from several directions.

Courtney took a step, and winced.

"Something wrong?" Billy said.

"I think I sprained something when I fell." Courtney took a few more steps, testing. "But I can manage."

At the tree line she looked back.

Marysville was crawling with creatures. Smoke and flames were rising from the gas station.

"Dear Lord, no!" Sally Ann gasped.

"What is it?" Billy said.

"Run!" Sally Ann said. "Run like you've never run before!"

They tried their best but the undergrowth was so thick, they hadn't gone more than twenty yards when the biggest explosion that Courtney ever heard shook the earth under their feet.

"Down!" Sally Ann bawled. "All of you!"

A series of blasts punctuated her cry, one after the other, attended by incredible sheets of flame shooting hundreds of feet into the air.

"The gas station went up!" Sally Ann shouted.

Courtney held Sansa and Gaga close. She didn't think they were in any danger. They were far enough away.

Then fiery objects began to rain from the sky. Some were the size of pebbles. Others a lot larger.

Sally Ann let out an "Ouch!" and swatted at her hair.

A burning 'something' thudded down almost at Courtney's feet.

Smaller explosions followed the first. The fierce rain continued but most fell farther away.

"Want to bet the fire spreads to some of the houses?" Billy said.

"Goodbye Marysville," Sally Ann said..

They stood, and Courtney cast about for zombies. She didn't see any. "Keep it quiet," she advised, "and follow me."

"Who died and made you leader?" Sally Ann said.

"Stay here if you want," Courtney said. She headed out, Sansa to one side, Gaga brushing her leg.

Willis was huddled in Sansa's arms, trembling.

The woods were a scary sight at night. There were too many dark places where things might be waiting to spring from ambush.

Twice Courtney heard the crackling of brush and stopped in her tracks. Whatever was responsible passed them by, and once the crackling faded, she resumed their flight.

In her estimation they had traveled half a mile when she halted and motioned for the others to cluster around.

"What's up?" Sally Ann said.

"Are you stopping for the night?" Billy asked.

"We've come far enough that we should be clear of the zombies," Courtney figured. "Let's head for the road. We're too closed in here in the forest."

"That's a good thing," Sally Ann said. "Makes it harder for the zombies or whatever to spot us."

"And for us to spot them."

"I have an idea," Billy said. "Why not just stay right where we are until the sun is up?"

Sansa broke her long silence, saying, "I don't like the woods."

"Me either, sweetie," Courtney said.

"On the road we're too vulnerable," Sally Ann said.

"I'm with Sal," Billy said. "Right here is safer."

A fierce howl proved him wrong.

Courtney whirled and clutched the revolver in both hands. She had never heard a zombie howl like that so it must be something else. Whatever it was, it wasn't more than a stone's throw away.

"What on earth?" Billy whispered.

Sansa's fingers dug into Courtney's arm.

Both dogs were staring intently into the trees, and both were shaking.

Courtney braced for the crash of brush and for something to attack them but anxious minutes crept by and nothing happened. The howl wasn't repeated.

"Maybe whatever it was is gone," Billy whispered.

"Hope you're right," Courtney said, "because we're heading for the road. And don't give me any of that 'we're safer' here crap."

To nip any argument, Courtney took Sansa's hand and headed in the direction of where the road should be.

Sally Ann said to hold up but Courtney kept going. Her nerves were rubbed raw. She was set to shoot at anything that moved.

It was impossible to be quiet. The undergrowth was too thick. Courtney worried that the crackle and cruch of their passage would draw some horror.

Courtney prayed that they hadn't gone through all they had for nothing. She hoped that they weren't on a wild goose chase, as her dad might have called it.

Incredibly, it was only days ago that Sally Ann's dad set up a radio in their kitchen. The kind of radio that received not just AM and FM, but shortwave and other bands too. It was while scouring the airwaves that they heard about a survivalist compound in northern Minnesota, a place where they might find shelter from the madness. 'Might', because they had no idea if the people who lived there would let them in. It could be they would get there, only to be refused entry.

"Psssst! Courts!" Billy whispered. "The road!"

Courtney blinked. She had been so deep in thought, she hadn't noticed. But there it was, a wide dark ribbon running straight and true.

Courtney was cautious. They mustn't blunder into the open. "Hold onto Sansa, will you?" she said to Sally Ann.

Sally reached over but Sansa shook her head and clung to Courtney's arm.

"I want to stay with you!"

"It will only be for a minute or two," Courtney assured her.

"I only want you."

"I don't bite, little one," Sally Ann said with a smile.

"You're not Courtney."

"Will I do?" Billy offered. "Courts and me have been friends since we were younger than you."

"Not you either," Sansa insisted.

Courtney was resigned to taking her but Billy hefted his rifle and strode past.

"Stay with your fan club, Courts. I'll make sure the coast is clear."

"Be careful."

Billy grinned. "I didn't know you cared."

Courtney smiled but she wasn't all that amused. Recently, to her amazement, Billy had confided that he liked her as more than a friend. He even went so far as to hint that he had been thinking about asking her to marry him.

Talk about shocks.

Never once, in all the years she knew him, did she think of him that way. They were buds. Plain and simple. Had been since grade school. She liked it that way. She wasn't into the idea of friends with benefits, or booty calls.

She had dated other guys but never anything serious. All the pressure that high schoolers were under to 'do it' rolled off of her like water off a duck. She didn't give a good damn what others did. Let them hump their brains out. It wasn't for her.

Nor had she given any thought to marriage. Oh, now and then she'd wonder how her life would play out and who she would end up with.

But Billy? One of her childhood friends?

No way.

Courtney gave her head a toss. Now wasn't the time to be thinking about things like that. Not when the night was filled with creatures out to kill them.

Billy was almost to the road. He looked back and waved.

Sally Ann came closer. "How are you holding up?"

"Just peachy," Courtney said.

"We need to find a place to stay for the night."

"The first house we come to....," Courtney began, and stopped.

Something was behind Sally Ann. Something that reared onto two legs and spread its arms wide.

CHAPTER 12

"Lookout!" Courtney bawled, and shoved Sally Ann out of the way. Caught off guard, Sally stumbled and fell, revealing that the thing Courtney believed was about to attack her....was a small black bear.

A young one, barely taller than Sally, and thinner than any bear Courtney ever saw. Instead of bareing its teeth, it whined like a puppy, dropped onto all fours, and did the last thing Courtney expected.

It ran off.

"What the hell?" Sally Ann said, rising and brushing herself off. "You didn't have to push me so hard."

"Next time I'll let whatever it is eat you," Courtney said in annoyance.

Sansa tugged on Courtney's arm and pointed.

Billy was over on the road, beckoning.

Courtney couldn't get out of the woods fast enough.

The road appeared empty. To the south, in the direction of Marysville, the sky was lit by the glow of fires. To the north, pale starlight lent a ghostly tint to the landscape.

"Not a zombie in sight," Billy said.

"Don't jinx us," Courtney said. She strode off up the middle of the road, Gaga padding at her side, Sansa quick-stepping to keep up.

"Hey, what's your rush?" Billy said, overtaking them. "Let's stick together, huh?"

Deceptive quiet had fallen. The woods seemed

serene but Courtney knew better. She constantly flicked her eyes right and left, her right hand always on her revolver.

"Any regrets, Courts?" Billy asked.

"Huh?" Courtney said, unsure what he meant.

"I regret I couldn't save my dad and mom," Billy said. "I regret I couldn't save the people at that camp we stayed at. Heck, I regret not being able to save Sal's dad."

"Where did all this come from?"

"Oh, I've been thinking, is all," Billy said. "Don't you have any regrets?"

Courtney did, in fact. She regretted not being nicer to her family before the world went to hell. She regretted not knowing what became of her parents and her sister and brother. She regretted not being smarter about things. Most of all, she regretted that Billy asked. "This is hardly the time."

"How often do we get to talk like this?" Billy said.

"Save it for when we don't have to worry about being torn to pieces or turned into one of the living dead."

"When will that be? A month from now? Six months?" Billy shook his head. "You ask me, we should open up to each other whenever we have the chance."

"Is that what you're doing?"

"I can't help it," Billy said. "After our talk the other day...."

"I knew it," Courtney cut him off. "I told you then and I'm telling you now. Drop it. We have too much on our minds as it is."

"I can't help it if I love you," Billy said.

Behind them, Sally Ann gave a sharp intake of breath. "Say what? Did I just hear what I think I heard?"

"As if it's a big surprise," Billy said. "You two must be the only ones at school who didn't know."

As much as Courtney wanted him to drop it, her curiosity got the better of her. "Wait a minute. Are you saying you told others?"

"I didn't have to," Billy said. "It was obvious."

"Not hardly," Courtney said, but a troubling seed took root, memories of things he had said over the years and incidents she hadn't given much thought.

"If World War Three hadn't come along," Billy had gone on, "I'd still be mooning over you and afraid to say anything for fear you'd throw it in my face."

"I would never....." was all Courtney got out.

"You're still not taking me serious, Courts," Billy said. "But I've known since third grade. The first time I saw you, I knew you were the one for me."

Astounded to her core, Courtney didn't know what to say.

"You honestly never suspected?"

"Billy," Courtney said, and not knowing what else to say, added, "Billy, Billy, Billy."

"You and me, Courts, it was meant to be. It's fine if you don't want to talk about it just now. But before we reach the compound, I'd like an answer. Do I have a shot or not? Do you feel even a little like how I feel about you?"

"Wow," Sally Ann said. "You two do realize it's the end of the world as we know it, right?"

"What's that got to do with anything?" Billy said.

Before Sally Ann could answer, several bright beams of light impaled them in a brilliant glare and a harsh voice called out, "Freeze or we'll shoot!"

Courtney's first reaction was to grab for her revolver.

It was the same reaction the others had. Billy started to level his rifle and Sally Ann tried to swing her shotgun up.

From out of the glare, men were on them. One shoved the muzzle of a rifle practically in Courtney's face. Another did the same with a pistol to Sally Ann.

They both turned to stone.

A third man slammed the butt of his rifle against Billy's temple. Billy collapsed.

"Didn't listen worth a damn," snarled the man who had shouted for them to freeze. He was holding a large utility flashlight.

Two more approached from either side, holding flashlights and guns.

"We've got babes!" the guy holding the rifle on Courtney exclaimed, and giggled like he was ten years old. "Hot damn!"

"Shut up, Floyd," the man with the utility flashlight said. "We don't want to scare them."

Floyd giggled some more.

The man who acted like their leader nudged Billy with a toe, then looked at Courtney and Sally Ann. "This how it is. You're ours, to do with as we please. We're taking you somewhere. Give us grief and we'll knock you out like doofus here and carry you, so don't waste our time by being stupid."

"How can you?" Sally Ann said. "What kind of people are you?"

The man stared at Sansa, who was cluthing Willis and peeking fearfully up their captors. "We got us a runt two." He paused. "Shoot the dogs."

Floyd swiveled his rifle toward Gaga, who was pressed against Courtney's legs. Instantly she swatted the barrel aside and bent over Gaga to protect her with her body.

"Don't you dare!"

"Get out of the way, girl," their leader said. "We don't have time for your nonsense with zombies all over the place."

"You try to shoot either dog and I'll fight you," Courtney said. "You might knock me out or you might kill me but I won't let you harm them."

"They're just dogs," the leader said.

"Don't you hurt Willis, mister!" Sansa said. "He's my friend."

"Hell," the leader said.

Another man with a flashlight turned it in the direction of Marysville. "Niles! Eaters on the way!"

Four zombies were shuffling toward them, the creature in the lead a broomstick with a jagged hole where its left cheek had been, exposing bone and teeth.

Niles drew one of a pair of semiautomatics he wore around his waist. "Damn it. Take care of them. Quietly. Then we'll take this bunch to the cabin."

"The dogs too?" a man asked.

"The stupid dogs too," Niles said. "For now."

Courtney didn't resist when Floyd took her revolver. She was watching three men who peeled away to deal with the creatures. They had it down pat. Each drew a long knife. As they neared the foremost zombie, one man stood in front of it, drawing the thing's attention, while another slipped to the side and stabbed it in the head. Neat and quick. In a heartbeat the zombie was dead---or dead again---on its feet. The other three were similarly dispatched.

"You're good at that," Sally Ann said.

"We're good at killing, period, girl," Niles said. "You'd be smart to remember that."

"You don't have to be so mean," Sansa spoke up.

"Grow up, kid," Niles said. "We do what we have to."

"You're just scavengers," Sally Ann said in contempt.

"Not another word out of you, bitch," Niles said. "Not until I say you can talk." He smirked at Sally Ann. "That is, unless you want to get by with fewer teeth."

"The same go for me?" Courtney said.

"Need you ask?" Niles retorted.

Two of the huskiest took hold of Billy, and Niles led them into the woods heading west.

The men turned off their flashlights and hiked under the starlight.

Any urge Courtney felt to try and escape was smothered by the rifle Floyd kept gouging into the small of her back. That, and Sansa and the dogs. She wouldn't abandon them, no matter what.

Niles stopped and waited for her to reach him and then fell in beside her. He made a show of looking her up and down.

Courtney had no need to ask why. Her skin crawled, and she silently vowed that if he tried to lay a hand on her, she would kill him, dead, dead, dead.

CHAPTER 13

As they hiked on, their captors talked in low tones.

Courtney learned a lot by paying close attention.

For starters, she learned some of their names. There was Niles, their leader. There was giggly-boy, Floyd. A guy with a beard, called Jenks, and a balding doughnut by the name of Rufus. Another, with a hook for a left hand, was called Leroy. A big slab of muscle was Bradley. She didn't hear the seventh man's name.

They all wore leather jackets or leather vests. On their backs was a large white paw with red claws that dripped blood. Which made perfect sense, because above each paw in large white letters was THE CLAWS MC.

They hadn't gone far when Billy came around. He muttered and stiffened and must have realized he was being held by two men and tried to break free.

"What the hell? Let go of me? What do you think you're doing?"

Billy struggled, but only until Niles held a pistol to his forehead.

"Listen up, boy," Niles said in his gravely voice. "I'd as soon splatter your brains. But we might have a use for you." He gestured at Courtney and Sally Ann. "Do as your lady friends are doing and behave and keep your mouth shut and you'll live longer."

Billy looked at Courtney and she nodded to indicate he should go along. He simmered down and marched along peacefully.

Niles returned to Courtney's side. "Is he your boyfriend, girl?"

"We've been friends since grade school," Courtney said.

"Just friends, huh? Good. That'll make things easier."

"Easier how?"

"You'll find out."

Behind Courtney, Floyd giggled.

"You're bikers, aren't you?"

Niles stared at her and for a few moments Courtney thought he was going to punch her for asking a simple question.

"Figured that out, did you?"

"Where are your motorcycles?"

"At the cabin," Niles said, and rubbed the back of his neck as if he had a kink. "We learned early on that our bikes draw those dead things likes garbage draws flies."

"The noise," Courtney said.

"Of course, you dumb bitch," Floyd spoke up.

"No need to insult me."

Niles had a smile like a shark's. "A bunch of strange men grab you and you have a gun in your spine and you're upset over that?"

Sally Ann said, "The Claws? I saw a news story about your bunch a year or so ago. Weren't you in a fight with some Hell's Angels or somebody like that?"

"Were we ever," Niles said, and several others laughed. "They were trying to muscle in on our territory for years."

"There's just the seven of you?" Sally Ann said.

"It's more like sixty," Niles replied. "But we're spread

out. Me and these boys were at Little Falls when everything went to hell. We needed a place to lie low. Somewhere away from the missiles and those dead suckers. I remembered my uncle's cabin."

"You're not safe there," Sally Ann said. "You're not safe anywhere."

"Says you," Niles said.

"Marysville was overrun by a huge swarm," Sally Ann informed him.

"A swarm?" Floyd giggled.

"Ask Courtney and Billy if you don't believe me."

Niles looked at Courtney. "That youre name, sweet cheeks?"

"My friend is telling the truth," Courtney said. "There was a huge number. A herd. An army. Whatever you want to call it."

"They go after people in the towns and cities," Niles said. "We're way out in the middle of nowhere."

"How many have you waylaid like you did us?" Sally Ann said.

Floyd responded before Niles could. "Waylaid? Where'd you learn to talk, girl? You one of those college brats."

"I'm in high school," Sally Ann said.

"Even better," Floyd said, and once again several of them laughed.

Courtney was trying to put on a front, to pretend she wasn't scared, but she was more worried about these creeps than she was about the zombies.

The end of the world kept getting worse and worse.

The cabin was no such thing.

Courtney didn't know why, maybe because she had

seen one on TV sometime, but the words that popped into her head when she laid eyes on it was, 'Swiss chalet'.

Twice the size of her family's house in Minneapolis, the peaked roof was a good three stories high. The front and backs---except for doors---were glass from top to bottom. The sides were composed of logs. A deck ran along the entire front, with chairs and a table and a grill with a cover over it.

To one side was a garage, the door open. Inside were motorcycles, dimly lit in the glow of a single small overhead bulb.

As they approached the front deck, a spotlight blazed bright.

The front door opened and out came a couple more Claws. One was young and skinny with a Mohawk and a gap where two of his upper front teeth should be. He leered at Courtney and Sally Ann. "Goody! Goody! Goody! You brought back some sweets for my sweet tooth!"

"Cool your tool, Spike," Niles said. "They're not to be touched until and when I say so."

"You're the leader, leader," Spike said, and tittered.

Floyd giggled as if he thought the comment was funny, too.

"Any trouble?" the other biker asked. He was wide across the chest, with gray hair and a salt-and-pepper beard.

"Not much, Gramps," Niles said.

Spike hooked his thumbs in his concho leather belt and swaggered to the steps. "I've got me an idea, bros. How about we have us a dog roast and for desert treat ourselves to the sugar pots?"

"I told you to cool your tool," Niles said.

"Hey, we could all stand a meal, and dog meat is as good as any other," Spike said.

Courtney balled her fists. "You touch one hair on our dogs...."

"And what, girlie?" Spike taunted. "You'll glare me to death?"

Some of the bikers laughed.

"Look," Sally Ann said, stepping up to Niles. "Does it have it be like this? Why can't you treat us right? Oh, sure, you can try to rape us..."

"Try?" Spike said, and snorted.

Sally Ann ignored him. "...but we'll fight like hell and you could end up killing one or both of us. And, sure, you can kill and eat our dogs but there's got to be better things to eat...."

Niles held up a hand, stopping her. "What's your point?"

"Why not try to get along? Why not treat us decent? We can cook for you, and whatever else around this place you don't like to do." She sniffed a few times. "Like wash your clothes, maybe."

"Give me a break," Floyd said. "Who cares about dirty clothes?"

"Then there's the place we're headed for," Sally Ann said. "Have you heard about it? A safe haven with a lot of people."

"What are you talking about?" Niles said.

"A survivalist compound," Sally Ann elaborated. "It's got high walls to keep the zombies out. And provisions."

"What the hell are provisions?" Spike said.

"Food and stuff," Niles said, sounding interested.

"Bet you're just making this up. Where'd you hear about this place?"

Courtney felt she should come to Sally Ann's defense. "On the radio. When we were in the Twin Cities. We caught a broadcast from a radio station. It mentioned the compound. Said anyone who could hear them should go there."

Spike let out with a bleat of mirth. "Yeah, right."

Billy broke his long silence. "I heard it to. So did Sal's father but he was killed. It's where we were headed."

"Survivalists?" Niles thoughtfully rubbed the stubble on his chin.

"You're not buying this crap, are you?" Spike said.

"I think they're telling the truth," Gramps put in.

"So do I," said the biggest one, Bradley.

"Makes three of us," Niles said.

"So what?" Spike snapped.

"Yeah, so what?" Floyd said.

Niles stared at each of them. "God, you two are dumb. I'll explain it to you later." He faced the rest and raised his arms to get their attention. "Listen up. No one is to touch our....guests. There are still cans of soup and whatever in the cupboard so if you're hungry grab a bite. We're having a meeting in about twenty minutes."

"Do we have a deal?" Sally Ann said.

"Let's just say you get to live a little longer while I think things over," Niles said.

"We'll take what we can get," Sally Ann said.

CHAPTER 14

"I hate this," Billy whispered. "I want to bash in their heads. Blow their brains out. Cut their throats."

"Calm down," Courtney said.

The three of them were restricted to the kitchen. A long marble counter separated it from a spacious living room. There was a fridge and a stove and oak cupboards, and off around a corner, in a nook, sat a large freezer.

Sally Ann had put the dogs by the freezer and blocked them in by placing a couple of chairs on their sides on the floor. "For their own good," she explained when Sansa objected. "The less those bikers see of them, the better."

Power to the chalet was being supplied by a generator in a shed. When Courtney stood by the back window, she could hear it running. But the sound was muffled and wouldn't carry far.

"I hate this," Billy continued to gripe.

"Give it a rest," Courtney said. Sally Ann was at the counter, her arms folded, watching the bikers. "I wonder what they're up to."

Courtney was curious about the same thing. All nine were together, either on chairs or sitting on the floor Niles was addressing them in low tones, and to a man, they hung on every word.

"What's that about," Billy said.

Courtney had an idea. "You two stand here and

pretend you're shooting the breeze."

"What are you going to do?" Billy asked.

Dropping flat, Courtney twisted around. Sally Ann and Billy gaped in surprise. Courtney put a finger to her lips, then quickly crawled past them until she came to the end of the counter.

Inching around it, she strained to hear.

".... all we'll ever need and it's ours for the taking," Niles was saying.

"How so?" Floyd said.

"This compound," Niles said. "These survivalists. How about we go there? How about we act all peaceful and get them to let us in? How about we bide our time and when the moment is right, we take over the place for ourselves?"

"I get you," Jenks said.

"I don't," Spike said. "What do we want with some stupid compound?"

"Use your brain for once, will you?" Niles said testily. "We have maybe two to three days of food left. Then what? We scrounge for more and bring it back. And do the same thing, week in and week out. And the whole time, we've got those damn dead things to worry about. What if one of those swarms shows up?"

"We take our bikes and cruise where the wind blows us," Leroy said.

"Yeah. Sure. With zombies and those pus-covered things and whatever else is out there waiting to rip us to shreds," Niles said. "How long do you think we'd last?"

"We're the Claws, bro," Spike said. "We'll kick anybody's ass."

Niles sighed. "And that green fog. You going to kick

its ass, too?" He shook his head. "Everything has changed, damn it. The world isn't like it was. We might last a while, but sooner or later we'll be done in like most everyone else. Unless...." he paused.

"Unless we take the compound from the survivalists so we'll have a safe place of our own," Gramps finished for him.

"They probably have food enough to last years," Bradley said.

"And stuff like gas masks and geiger counters," Niles said.

Spike rubbed his cheek. "So you're saying that we make nice for a while and let the cuties lead us there, then kill however many we have to so we can take the place over?"

"You're slow but you get there," Niles said.

"It could be our base," Gramps said. "Live there and roam the countryside for whatever else we need."

"A sweet setup," Jenks said.

"But that means we don't get to lay a finger on those young fluffs," Spike said.

"Not until we take over the compound," Niles said.

"So what if we have to put on an act for a while," Gramps said. "It's no big deal."

"Well, hell," Spike said.

"Everyone has to agree," Niles said. "If you like the plan, nod."

Courtney risked a peek. One by one they nodded. Last, reluctantly, Spike did, too. She supposed she should be happy that she and her friends were being spared.

Courtney barely had time to scramble back to Sally Ann and Billy, and stand up, than Niles and Gramps came to the counter.

"We've decided to go see this compound for ourselves," Niles announced. "What with everything gone to hell, it's dog eat dog out there."

"You better not eat Willis," Sansa said.

"That's not what I meant, kid," Niles said. "We need to be somewhere there's less chance of us being eaten."

Gramps nodded. "Hopefully, these survivalists will let us in."

Billy opened his mouth to say something but Sally Ann beat him to it with, "They should. The radio made it sound as if they would."

Which Courtney knew was an outright lie.

"So here's how it will be," Niles said. "You keep to yourselves. Don't get in our faces. Pick a room for the three of you to sleep in tonight. We'll head out tomorrow about noon." He started to turn. "One more thing. We don't have bikes to spare. Each of you will have to ride double with one of us."

"I'd rather walk," Billy said.

"You sure try a man's patience, asshole," Niles said. "But if you want to try and make it there on your own, be my guest."

"He'll ride double," Courtney said. "He's just grumpy from being hit on the head."

Niles motioned at Gramps and they rejoined their friends.

No sooner were they out of earshot than Courtney whirled on Billy. "When will you stop being so pig-headed? she whispered, and went on before he could respond. "These bozos are our best bet of reaching the compound alive. Think about it. On their bikes we can get there in two days, tops...."

"Depending," Sally Ann said.

"....so play along until we're there," Courtney advised Billy. "I'd hate to lose you after all we've been through."

Billy brightened. "Really?"

Courtney knew he was thinking about his confession of love for her. He confirmed it by what he said next.

"Then there's hope for me yet."

Courtney sighed and took Sansa's hand and went around to the nook. She moved a chair so they could step through. Sinking down with her back to the wall, she petted Gaga.

Sansa picked up Willis and hugged him, his little tongue licking her like mad. "I hate that they talked about eating him."

"They're buttheads," Courtney said.

Sansa laughed. "I'm glad I'm with you. I'd be so scared if I wasn't."

"Sally Ann and Billy will protect you," Courtney assured her.

"Do you like Billy?"

The blunt question caught Courtney off guard. "We've been friends since forever."

"No," Sansa said. "Do you *like* him? You know. Boy, girl stuff?"

"Aren't you a little young for that?"

"Oh, eww," Sansa said. "I'm talking about you, not me. He likes you. Do you like him?"

"If by like you mean love, I'm not sure," Courtney said. "We're not boyfriend and girlfriend. We're just friends. He'd like to be more, but...."

"What?"

"I don't know," Courtney said. "Maybe if he'd told me how much he cared a week ago, before the missiles and the bombs, I'd have given it a try." She bowed her head and Gaga nuzzled her. "Now, I just don't know."

"I'm never going to fall in love," Sansa declared with absolute conviction.

"Is that so?"

Sansa nodded. "I know about kissing and things. It's yucky. I'd kiss a frog before I'd kiss a boy."

Courtney snickered.

"I'm serious," Sansa said. "I'm never having a boyfriend. I'm never getting married. I'm never having kids."

"Have your life all worked out, I take it?"

"I did," Sansa said, and became sad. "Until all of this terrible stuff happened. How about you?"

"I was taking it day by day," Courtney admitted. "I didn't have any plans. My parents wanted me to go to college but I was like, why bother? Why put myself in debt so I can hold a dull job somewhere?" She rubbed Gaga's neck. "Life for me was mostly a bore. School. My family. I just didn't care." She closed her eyes as images of those times washed over her. "God, I was stupid. A good life was right there in front of me and I didn't see it."

"You see it now?"

"I sure as hell do."

"You sound mad?"

"I sure as hell am," Courtney said.

"There's not much you can do about it now though, huh?" Sansa said.

Courtney almost burst into tears.

CHAPTER 15

Courtney was nervous about the motorcycles. They were so loud, she feared their combined din would draw shambling dead from all over.

She was riding double with Niles. Not that she was given a choice.

Sally Ann had to ride double with Gramps. Billy was with Jenks. The really big biker, Bradley, offered to take Sansa. At first Courtney was hesitant but Bradley treated the girl as nice as could be. From comments he dropped, Courtney gathered that he had a young girl of his own somewhere.

The dogs were another matter.

Spike and Floyd were for leaving Gaga and Willis behind. Several other Claws agreed but Courtney flat-out told them that if they didn't take the dogs, she'd refuse to go. When Spike laughed and said the Claws would force her, she vowed to fight them every foot of the way from then on.

Niles intervened. The dogs were coming along. Courtney was responsible for Gaga. Sally Ann brought Willis.

So for three hours now, as the Claws roared steadily northward along a series of back roads they knew like the backs of their hands, Courtney held tight to Gaga, who wouldn't stop trembling. It was awkward and uncomfortable and Courtney's arms were growing tired.

The Claws rode two abreast. Across from Niles was Gramps. Now and again Courtney and Sally Ann would catch each other's eyes and Sally would smile encouragement.

Courtney's own spirits were low. Despite heir best efforts, each day found them deeper in an unending nightmare. She supposed she should be grateful that the Claws were playing at hands off for the time being. But that would change when they reached the compound.

The day was overcast---as every day had been since the war. Instead of clouds, the sky was a sickly blanket of yellows and browns and greys.

And as was often the case, there was a faintly toxic smell to the air.

The roar of the cyles seemed to shake the ground. Several times Courtney spotted zombies near the road but the bikers swept by before the creatures could reach them.

Abandoned vehicles were fairly common. According to Sally Ann, something called an EMP had destroyed the electronics and brought a lot of cars and trucks to a stop.

The Claws expertly avoided every obstacle.

Courtney had to hand it to them. If there was one thing they did well, it was how they handled their heavy machines. They swerved and braked so smoothly, it was as if they and their bikes were one.

By Courtney's reckoning it was close to noon when the Claws swept around a curve---and the road ahead was blocked by a large creature.

Niles applied his brakes so hard, his cycle swerved, nearly causing Courtney to lose her grip on Gaga. The other bikers did the same, Spike coming within a few inches of slamming into Leroy.

"Hell no!" Gramps hollered.

It was a black bear. Or had been, before the war. Huge for its kind, most of its fur was gone, replaced by scabrous flesh and scores of putrid sores that oozed a yellowish-green pus. Its eyes, once brown, were now as red as blood. Part of an ear and a cheek had been eaten away by the chemical cloud that had transformed the bear into a living monster.

Woods hemmed the road on either side, the trees so packed that riding between them on a big bike would be impossible.

"Turn around!" Niles shouted, waving an arm over his head. "Hurry! Hurry!"

There wasn't enough room.

And there wasn't enough time.

Niles and Gramps were starting to turn their cycles when the mutated bear gave voice to a gurgling bellow of mad rage, and came at them like an out-of-control express train.

Courtney acted as fast as she could. Sliding her right leg over and around, she threw herself off the Harley, clutching Gaga close. Gaga, panicked, struggled to break free. Courtney had no choice but to let go. As she did, she stumbled, tripped, and fell.

Sansa screamed.

Billy yelled something.

Flat on her back, Courtney saw Niles grab at a pistol. His bike was halfway around, broadside to the bear. He tried to aim but the mutate slammed into him with such force, both he and his bike were smashed to the asphalt. Niles lost his hold on his pistol, which went skidding, and lost his head, literally, when the mutate swung a large paw----and severed Niles's head from his body.

Gramps was frantically attempting to turn his bike, Sally Ann recoiling in fear.

The mutate looked over at them, and then down at Courtney---and lunged toward her.

Courtney's doom was framed by the gaping maw of an animal driven berserk by man-made chemicals. Razor teeth, dripping saliva, filled her vision.

In that instant a shot boomed.

Floyd had unslung his rifle and fired before any of the others could resort to their own guns. His bike was only a few yards from Niles, and he frantically worked the bolt to feed a new round into the chamber.

The slug had taken the bear in the neck. Gore and blood erupted from the exit wound, but the shot seemed to have no other effect. With a horrendous roar, the bear forgot about Courtney and charged Floyd. He was steadying his rifle for a second shot when the creature tore into him with its foreclaws flashing and its teeth snapping.

Floyd was flayed alive, reduced to bone in mere seconds, his ribs and parts of his skull gleaming white. His scream was cut short.

Gramps took advantage of the bear's distraction to straighten his Harley and race on down the road instead of trying to turn around. He swept past the mutate, Sally Ann clinging tight to Willis.

Courtney took advantage, too. Flipping onto her belly, staying low, she started toward the trees, stopping when she heard Sansa wail in fear.

Bradley had been trying to turn his cycle and gotten it almost around when it stopped cold. The back end was toward the bear.

The back end, and Sansa.

Her cry brought the bear's head up from where it had been savaging Floyd's chest. Flesh and skin splattered its jaw as it stepped over Floyd's body toward Bradley's bike.

The big biker hadn't noticed. He was trying to restart his Harley.

Courtney heaved erect.

Other Claws were fleeing back the way they came.

Her young face twisted in terror, Sansa scrambled off Bradley's bike.

In those brief moments, Courtney was up and flying. She reached Sansa and grabbed for her arm.

The bear was almost on top of them. Rearing onto its hind legs, it slavered and snarled.

Courtney had nowhere to go. Bradley's bike blocked their retreat. The pus-oozing monstrosity was in front of them.

The thing cocked an arm to swing and Courtney bent over Sansa to shield the girl with her own body.

"Leave her be!"

Out of nowhere Billy was there, wielding a large knife. Heedless of the danger to himself, he rushed in and hacked and stabbed at the mutate.

"Get out of here, Courts! Go! Go! Go!'

Courtney didn't need to be urged twice. Scooping Sansa up, she ran into the woods. But she only went a few yards and stopped. "Billy! Come on!"

He was still battling. His left arm was torn from his shoulder to his elbow but he was gamely trying to hold the bear at bay.

Another biker---Spike---took off down the road.

Billy spun to run but the bear clipped him and sent him tumbling. It started after him, then saw Bradley still trying to kick-start his Harley.

The big biker's back was to the mutate. He never saw it close on him. Probably the first inkling he had that he was its new prey was when its curved claws ripped into his back at the base of his neck. Bradley shrieked as those same claws raked his spine clear down to his waist, leaving bloody furrows in their wake.

Keeping hold of Sansa, Courtney ran to Billy. She used her other arm to help him stagger to his feet.

"I can manage," he mumbled in obvious agony.

"Move, damn you!" Courtney bawled.

They fled, Billy tottering, Sansa clinging to Courtney's leg and impeding her. Ten...twenty....twenty-five yards they covered, Courtney expecting the bear to be after them at any moment. She led them around a pine and dropped to her knees. "Get down!" she whispered.

Billy doubled over, clutching his arm.

Sansa buried her face in Courtney's side.

To the north and south, in the distance, bike engines thrummed. The Claws, making their getaways.

Courtney peered through the pine's branches. She saw three bikes down. She saw Niles' headless body and what was left of Floyd and Bradley crumpled across the tank of his his fallen bike.

She didn't see the bear anywhere.

Then she heard a growl behind her.

CHAPTER 16

Courtney spun, wishing she had a weapon but prepared to fight tooth and nail to protect little Sansa.

But it was Gaga, crouched low and glaring toward the road. Gaga growled a second time.

Courtney turned toward the road, anticipating the worst.

The bear was loping north along the trees. In its mouth was Niles's head.

Courtney watched until the creature went around a bend. The second it was out of sight, she was on her feet. "Stay here," she told Sansa and Billy, and sprinted to the road.

One of Niles's pistols lay in a pool of blood. She grabbed it and wiped it on her jeans. She also undid the belt buckle to Niles's gunbelt, and strapped it around her waist. The other pistol was still in its holster.

Next she collected Floyd's rifle and Bradley's shotgun. In Floyd's jacket was a box of ammo. She also helped herself to a bandolier Bradley had worn

As an afterthought, Courtney checked the saddlebags on Bradley's bike. They contained a spare shirt and socks and other stuff. She snatched the shirt out.

She straightened to return to the others and discovered they hadn't listened. Sansa and Billy, with Gaga trailing after, had followed her.

Billy still had his right hand pressed to his left arm. Grimacing, he said, "We need is to get out of here. The bikers who ran off will come back."

Courtney held up the shotgun and the rifle. "That's why I got these."

"We should stick to the woods for the time being," Billy said. Grunting in pain, he headed back in.

Sansa was nervously shifting her weight from foot to foot. "That's smart, isn't it? So we're not spotted?"

Courtney nodded. She hated that they were separated from Sally Ann. But it couldn't be helped.

About twenty feet in, Billy sank down with his back to an oak. His left arm had stopped bleeding but was covered with drying blood. "Not my year," he said.

"Sorry?" Courtney said, kneeling beside him.

"Hurt my leg, my head, now this."

"Let me take a look."

Courtney gingerly pried at his sleeve. The bear's claws had raked him good but not so deep that he would lose the use of his arm. "I'll bandage you. Looks like you should be able to use your arm okay."

"Do what you can," Billy said.

Courtney tore the shirt she had taken from the saddlebags into strips. It was harder than she imagined it would be. She had to use her teeth for extra leverage.Once they were tied tight, she nodded and said, "That will have to do."

Billy experimented moving his arm. Up. Down. Right. Left. "Not bad, Courts," he said, offering a wan smile. "You'd make a good nurse."

"Not hardly," Courtney said. She couldn't stand to be around sick people.

Billy placed his hand on her shoulder. "Thanks. You're the best friend any guy ever had."

"Don't make more of it than there is," Courtney said,

worried he would wax romantic. "We should keep going. We have to find Sally."

"Gramps and her are probably miles away by now," Billy said.

"We don't know that," Courtney said. "And I'm going, whether you do or not." Harsh words, but necessary.

"How about you, kid?" Billy said to Sansa. "You up for this?"

"They have Willis."

Billy sighed and propped his good arm against the oak so he could stand. "Lead on, ladies," I'll be right behind you.

"First," Courtney said, holding out the rifle and shotgun. "Which will it be?"

"The shape my arm is in, the rifle will have less kick," Billy said.

Courtney assumed the lead. She stayed only a dozen feet from the road, alert for the mutated bear, or anything else.

Past the bend was a half-mile straightaway, likewise bounded by forest.

There was no sign of anything or anyone.

They were well along the straight stretch when Sansa said Courtney's name, and stopped. "Do you hear that?"

A moment later, Courtney did.

The quiet was broken by the growing thunder of motorcycle engines.

"It's some of those bad men," Sansa said. "They're coming back."

Courtney quickly moved a few yards deeper into the woods, and crouched. She told Sansa to lie flat and hold onto Gaga.

Billy was moving slow. He leaned his good shoulder against a tree and awkwardly worked the bolt of his rifle.

"What do you think you're doing?" Courtney said. "Let them go by."

"Why not do them in here and now?" Billy said. "Spare us the trouble if we run into them later."

"You're in no condition for a fight," Courtney remarked.

We can do it," Billy said. He braced the rifle against the tree and aligned the sights.

"No. Not with Sansa so close," Courtney said.

"Have her move farther away if you're worried she'll take a stray bullet," Billy said.

"No, damn it. She doesn't leave our sight. Not with all the zombies and whatnot."

Billy looked over. "Take her in farther if you want to. Me, I'm picking them off if I can."

The cycles were a lot louder. Movement on the road to the south showed how near they were.

Against her better judgement Courtney raised the shotgun. She mentally crossed her fingers that there weren't more than three or four Claws.

As luck would have it, there were two.

Spike and Jenks were riding side by side, Spike hunched forward, his face intent.

The pair were going at least fifty.

Billy took a deep breath, and fired.

Spike jerked and swerved but didn't go down. Gunning his engine, he swept forward.

Jenks slowed and looked toward the woods.

Courtney stroked the shotgun's trigger. She had

forgotten about the recoil. The upward sweep of the barrel partially blocked her view of the blast that caught Jenks in the shoulder and neck and flung him off his bike. He cried out as he tumbled and then lay still.

Billy ran toward the road while trying to work the rifle's bolt. His hurt arm hampered him.

"Don't show yourself!" Courtney yelled, running after him.

Billy paid her no mind. Hastening out of the trees, he pointed his rifle to the north, and swore.

Her nerves blaring, Courtney bounded into the open and brought her shotgun level.

Spike's motorcycle was in the middle of the road not sixty feet away. The kickstand was down, and Spike was nowhere to be seen.

Courtney glanced right and left. They had blundered, badly. "Get to cover!" she cried.

Billy was slow to react. He began to back up.

Courtney was frantic with worry but they gained the trees and ducked down.

"Where....?" Billy whispered.

"Beats me," Courtney said.

"Maybe my shot did him in," Billy said. "He made it off his bike but collapsed. One of us should go have a look."

"And if it's trick?"

"I'll go and you watch my back."

Courtney thought his plan sucked. Before she could say anything, Gaga whined and pressed against her leg. "Not now," Courtney whispered, and gently gave the dog a light push. "Go back to...." Apprehension shot through her and she swiveled on her heels and gasped, "Dear Lord, no!"

"Hi there," Spike said.

He was crouched behind Sansa, a hand clamped over her mouth, using her as a shield. His other hand held a small semiautomatic pressed to her forehead.

Sansa's face was drained of blood, her eyes pools of mute appeal.

Billy shifted around and went to point his rifle.

"I wouldn't, boy," Spike warned. A blood stain marked his shoulder, and he appeared to be in considerable pain.

"Damn," Billy said.

Spike smirked, then scowled. "You put a slug in me, boy. I owe you, bigtime."

"Let Sansa go," Courtney said. She didn't have a clear shot. Even if she did, with Sansa that close to him, she didn't dare use the shotgun.

"Be serious," Spike said.

"You harm that girl....," Billy said.

"Spare me your bluster," Spike said. "She's my insurance you'll do as I say."

"What is it you want?" Courtney asked.

"Oh, come on," Spike said. "You really need to ask?" His eyes were shards of flint. "I want you to lay your guns down and stand with your hands in the air. I want you to turn your backs to me and stay still as hell until I say different. If you don't, this little sweetie will take two in the brainpan and we let the chips fall where they may." He paused. "Which will it be?"

CHAPTER 17

Courtney hated having to give in. She had no choice, though, with Sansa's life in peril. She set the shotgun at her feet, then straightened with her arms straight up. "There."

"Turn around," Spike said.

Her skin prickling, Courtney did.

"Now it's your turn, boy," Spike growled.

"Like hell," Billy said.

"Didn't you hear me?" Spike said. "This brat is as good as dead if you don't."

"And Courts and I are as good as dead if we do."

Billy was holding the rifle at his waist, leveled at the Claw.

"Billy," Courtney said anxiously. "We have to do as he wants."

Billy shook his head. "He's not as smart as he thinks he is. If he shoots her, I shoot him."

"You'd risk this brat's life for a chance at me?" Spike said.

Billy nodded.

"Well, then," Spike shrugged and smiled as if it amused him---and as he smiled, he shoved Sansa toward Billy.

"Don't shoot!" Courtney cried.

Billy fired.

For a heart-stopping moment, Courtney thought he had shot Sansa. But no, Sansa wasn't hit. Nor, apparently, was Spike, who surprised Courtney by diving into a roll and darting around a pine and out of sight.

Courtney scooped up the shotgun as Billy worked the bolt on his rifle.

"Where'd he get to?"

Courtney was covering the pine. "More important," she said, "is why didn't he shoot?"

"Huh?" Billy said.

"He could have shot Sansa or you or me. Yet he didn't."

"He didn't want to take the risk of me getting him," Billy said. "So he lit out."

Courtney would be the last person in the world to compliment Spike, but she had to be honest. "No, I don't think that's it. I don't think he was afraid."

"Then why?"

"I wish I knew," Courtney said.

Sansa, trembling in fear, had moved behind her, and was holding onto Gaga. "What do we do?".

"We go after him," Billy said. "Hunt him down."

"You're in no condition to hunt anybody," Courtney said. "And we're not risking Sansa's life a second time. We get out of here while we can. Head north after Sally Ann."

"And Willis," Sansa said.

"There's two of us and one of him," Billy said stubbornly.

"Damn it," Courtney said. "Use your head. He could pick us off now if he wanted." She would swear unseen eyes were on them. But she was at a loss to explain what Spike was up to.

"Every time we turn around," Billy said, "we're

running from someone or something."

"We're still breathing." Courtney said. "You go first."

To her relief, Billy didn't argue. His hurt arm hung limp as he retreated toward the road. "Come on, then."

Courtney held the shotgun ready to shoot. "What are you up to?" she said to the woods. "Can't you just leave us be?"

From off in the shadows came a low laugh.

"I knew you were out there," Courtney said. When she got no response, she slowly retreated, saying, "If you have any sense, you'll go your own way. We're not worth the bother."

She doubted Spike would reply. But she was wrong. "One of you is."

Courtney couldn't pinpoint where he was hiding. She continued to back off until she was out of the trees.

Billy and Sansa were waiting. Billy looked worse.

"How are you holding up?"

"Fine," Billy said. He gestured. "Let's get while the getting's good."

Courtney didn't take her gaze off the woods. They came to Spike's motorcycle and Billy stepped up to it, smirking.

"What are you doing?" Courtney said.

"What does it look like?"

"Don't."

Billy glanced at her. "We damage it, he has to come after us on foot." He raised his leg.

"We don't damage it," Courtney said, "we'll hear him coming from half a mile away."

As if to bolster her point, the metallic throb of cycle engines rumbled to the north.

"That must be Gramps and the Claw that went with

him," Billy said. "They're coming back."

"And Sally Ann was riding with Gramps," Courtney said.

"Now we have them to take on and Spike lurking in the trees," Billy said. "Great. Just great. What next?"

The underbrush crackled and a zombie shuffled into the open.

Billy raised his rifle but Courtney pushed the barrel down and ran at the zombie. Thankfully, it was a slow one. It raised its bony finger toward her but she sidestepped and slammed the barrel of her shotgun against its temple. It stumbled, and she struck again, knocking it down. It tried to rise and she kicked it in the head, over and over, her foot hurting but she didn't care, until finally the thing stopped moving.

"Damn, that was fierce!" Billy said. "Why didn't you just let me shoot it?"

"Gramps might hear," Courtney said. "Come on." She broke into a jog. They needed to put distance between them and Spike's bike.

Courtney held onto Sensa, who gamely kept up. When they had gone thirty yards or so, she ducked into the woods and crouched.

Billy was grimacing and holding his hurt arm close to his side. He sank to one knee, placed his rifle's stock on the ground, and leaned on it. "Why?" he puffed.

The approaching roar of the motorcycles to the north was a lot louder.

"So we can take Gramps and whoever is with him by surprise," Courtney said. "And rescue Sally Ann."

"Ah," Billy said. He was red in the face and caked with sweat.

Courtney put a hand to his forehead. "You're

burning up."

"Not feeling all that good," Billy admitted.

Courtney hoped an infection wasn't setting in. They had no way of treating it. But first problems first. She told Sansa to lie flat, then took up a position behind a tree as close to the road as she dared without exposing herself.

Billy followed her example, bracing his good shoulder against the trunk.

"Let me do this," Courtney said.

"Every gun helps." Billy wiped his sweaty forehead with his sleeve.

"We need to get this over with quick so I can tend to you," Courtney said.

Billy smiled with affection. "Thanks, Courts, for being my friend."

"Right back at you." Courtney said, and focused on the road, specifically on the bend that Gramps and whoever was with him would soon come around.

"I mean it," Billy said, his voice choked with emotion.

Courtney glanced at him. "Now's not the time, doofus."

Billy said something that was drowned out by the racket the two motorcycles made as they swept around the bend.

Gramps was in the lead. Behind him came Rufus, the human doughnut. They saw Spike's bike in the middle of the road up ahead, and slowed.

Exactly as Courtney hoped they would do. She pointed her shotgun at Gramps but needed him closer to be sure. "You take Rufus."

"Will do," Billy said.

The two bikers came on at a crawl, both looking right and left, suspiciously.

Come on! Courtney thought. Just a little closer! The wait frayed at her nerves. She itched to cut loose.

"Hey," Billy whispered. "Where's Sal?"

Only then did Courtney realize that Sally Ann---and Willis---weren't on the back of Gramps's bike.

"What did they do with her?" Billy said.

Gramps and Rufus were near enough now but Courtney was so shocked that Sally Ann was missing that she raised her head and looked toward the bend.

Gramps spotted her. He pointed and yelled and swerved his bike toward the other side of the road. Rufus did the same.

Billy fired but must have missed because Rufus didn't so much as flinch.

Recovering her wits, Courtney aimed at Gramps's broad back. She stroked the trigger but nothing happened. She had forgotten to feed a fresh shell into the chamber after she shot Jenks. Quickly, she remedied her mistake but by then Gramps and Rufus had threaded their bikes into the trees, and jumped off.

"Can't anything ever go right?" Billy said in frustration while once again working the bolt on his rifle. "Now there are three of them out there."

"We should get away while we can," Courtney said. What with Billy sick and Sansa to think of and being outnumbered, it was the smart thing to do.

"I hate running," Billy reiterated.

"I'd hate being dead." Courtney turned and held out her hand to Sansa. "Let's go, little one."

Gaga suddenly swiveled her head toward the woods at their back.

Courtney looked, and felt a wave of cold spike through her.

Spike was sneaking toward them.

CHAPTER 18

Spike was still a ways off, darting from cover to cover.

"Keep low," Courtney said, and angled deeper into the woods, away from the road and Gramps and Rufus, and away from Spike. She tried to keep an eye on him but lost him in the underbrush.

When she had gone far enough to deem it safe, Courtney stopped to get her bearings.

Billy was literally drenched with sweat and blinking his eyes a lot.

"You look terrible," Courtney couldn't help saying. "Let's rest."

"We haven't gone far enough," Billy said. "Keep going."

Against her better judgement, Courtney pushed on. She went as fast as the growth---and Sansa---allowed.

A timber-covered hill reared and she went around it.

On the other side lay a hollow. Oval-shaped, it was as if a giant scoop had dug out the earth.

"In here." Courtney descended the short incline, then helped Sansa down.

Billy stood on the lip, swaying. His face was red and the whites of his eyes had a peculiar yellow tinge. "God, I feel awful."

"Rest, for heaven's sake." Courtney held up an arm to help him and he surprised her by taking it and letting her. Ordinarily, he would want to do it himself.

Billy sank to the grass, lay on his back, and groaned.

"I'm burning up, Courts."

Courtney's heart skipped a beat when she checked his forehead. His skin was so hot, it was like touching the burner on a stove. "We need to find water."

"I need more than that," Billy said thickly.

"I'll go look for some," Courtney offered.

"Do me a favor first," Billy said. "Check my arm. It feels really strange."

"Let me see." Moving to his other side, Courtney knelt. She carefully pried at his shirt, her nose crinkling at the foul odor that rose. His arm wasn't swollen much, but like his eyes, it was a sickly shade of yellow. She undid the bandage, and had to cover her mouth and nose with her other hand, the smell was so rank.

Festering sores had formed around and between the claw marks. From them oozed a thick yellowish-green pus.

Courtney felt her stomach heave and swallowed the bitter bile back down.

"How bad is it?" Billy asked. He tried to raise his head to see but he was too weak. "I can't tell much."

"It's......" Courtney was about to say 'not too bad' but she hated to lie to him.

"It feels like I'm on fire and yet ice-cold at the same time," Billy said. "How can that be?" He coughed, and yellow spit dribbled from a corner of his mouth.

"You're infected," Courtney stated the obvious. She sat back, racking her brain as to what she should do. Going for help was out of the question. She didn't dare leave them alone. Billy was in no shape to protect Sansa should the bikers or something else happen along.

"Courts?" Billy said. His eyes were closed and he was starting to breathe heavily. "My chest feels funny."

Shaking herself, Courtney took his hand in both of hers. "I'm here," she said. Even as she bent over him, mucus dribbled from his nose.

"Don't go, okay?" Billy said.

"I won't."

"Do you remember....," Billy said, and shivered. "Do you remember when we were in grade school? How I'd pull your hair and tease you?"

"I remember," Courtney said, her throat constricted.

"I did it because I liked you."

"I know."

"And in middle school? How I liked to hang with you at lunch? And that study hall we took together?"

"You've always been a good friend."

"I have, haven't I?" A slow smile spread across Billy's face. His chest rose and fell deeply with each breath.

"I'm so sorry," Courtney said softly.

"For what?"

"When you told me that you loved me...."

"Oh, that." Billy opened his eyes. "I wish the stupid war hadn't happened. I wish we could have lived out our lives how I'd hoped." He shook from head to toe. "I wish...."

When he didn't go on, Courtney bent lower. "Billy?"

He didn't answer.

And he never would.

How long she sat there crying, Courtney couldn't say. Several times she felt Sansa tug at her arm and say her name but she didn't respond. She sat with her head bowed and her heart heavy, and cried as she had never wept in her life.

Billy had been her friend. One of her very best. They

had known each other for so long, done so many fun things together, he was as close to her as anyone. Now he was gone. Torn from her, and from life, by the madness spawned by those in high places. By power-hungry bastards who had plunged the world into chaos. Creeps who destroyed untold millions. Who caused no end of suffering and horror. And why? Because they thought they had the right to lord it over everyone else. Because they didn't give a good damn about anyone or anything except for themselves and their screwball politics.

Now, because of despicable people like that, she had lost someone else dear to her.

Reaching out, Courtney tenderly touched Billy's shoulder. The yellow pus continued to seep from his sores and she was careful not to touch them. For all she knew, the toxins could be absorbed through the skin.

Time passed, and at last she had no more tears to shed. Her cheeks were slick, her neck wet. Her eyes, though, were dry, and smarting. Clearing her throat, she roused and gazed about.

Overhead, the unnatural cloud cover. All around, the whisper of the wind in the woods, along with an occasional animal cry. At that instant a shriek torn from a throat in no wise human came from far off.

It was cool and deceptively peaceful in the hollow. Courtney looked over to find Sansa curled on her side, sound asleep, an arm over Gaga, the pair cuddled together for warmth.

Courtney sidled beside them and lay down, protectively curling her arm above the pair. She was suddenly weary to her marrow. She closed her eyes, and just-like-that she was out to the world. A tiny voice deep in her mind warned her to stay alert, that there was no telling what might come across them in the dead of night. She couldn't stop herself. She drifted off and slept the sleep of the dead.

A chattering sound roused her from the depths of the abyss. She struggled to wake up, blinking in the dull grey of a new day.

Sansa was still asleep. Gaga was awake but lying quietly.

Above them, the chattering was repeated.

Feeling so sluggish she could hardly move, Courtney twisted her head around.

A pine grew near the lip of the hollow. From up a high branch, a squirrel vented its annoyance at their intrusion into its world.

Courtney closed her eyes and was settling back when it occurred to her that maybe something else had agitated it.

Sitting up, Courtney scanned the circle of trees. She rose into a crouch, her legs protesting, and slowly unfurled until she could peer over the top.

At first everything appeared normal. Just the trees and the undergrowth and the silly squirrel.

Then some brush rustled and a dark shape appeared, too indistinct to make out.

Courtney realized she had left the shotgun lying near Billy, and turned to reclaim it. And froze.

The undergrowth had parted and out strode a cougar. Tilting its head, it sniffed a few times.

Courtney tensed. It appeared to be normal. Even so. she had heard news stories about cougar attacks. Not a lot of them, but if this one was hungry enough, who knew? She eased toward the shotgun, then saw that

Billy's rifle was closer. By stretching her arm as far as she could, she snagged the barrel and dragged the weapon toward her.

The cougar's ears twitched and it looked down into the hollow.

Courtney took aim. As fast as she was, the big cat was faster. It was gone in the blink of an eye, melting into the undergrowth as silently as its shadow.

To say Courtney was relieved was an understatement. She was sick of fighting, sick of having to kill. "Thank you, God," she whispered.

"Courtney?"

Sansa sat up, sleepily rubbing her eyes. She blinked, and beamed, and was on her feet hugging Courtney's legs. "Are you all right? Are you yourself again?"

"I'm me," Courtney assured her.

Gaga rose, and tried to press between them.

"I'm sorry about Billy," Sansa said.

Courtney swallowed.

"What do we do now? Keep going to that place up north?"

"It's as good as anywhere."

"Do you think we'll make it?"

"Let's hope," Courtney said.

CHAPTER 19

It wasn't smart to try and take the shotgun and the rifle, both. It would be awkward. Neither had a sling. Lugging them would tire Courtney more readily and she needed her strength for the miles of hiking ahead.

Courtney chose the shotgun. At close range it was a cannon. Besides, she wasn't a marksman. Or markswoman.

Sansa offered to bring the rifle but Courtney told her to leave it.

"I really want to," Sansa insisted.

"It would slow you down," Courtney said, giving Gaga an affectionate pat.

"You have a gun. I want one," Sansa wouldn't let it drop.

"It weighs more than you think," Courtney tried again.

"Let me try," Sansa said. "I want to be able to protect myself."

"Fine. But when you can't carry it anymore, just set it down. We'll find something easier for you."

The rifle was as long as Sansa was tall. She looked comical holding it but Courtney didn't say anything.

Spike's bike was gone. Nor was there any sign of Gramps or Rufus

"Where you think they got to?" Sansa asked.

"No telling," Courtney said. But she would bet they had headed north to the compound, which meant there was a good chance she would run into them again.

An eerie stillness prevailed. The only sounds were the slap of their shoes on the asphalt.

No zombies appeared.

No mutates, either.

Courtney constantly scoured the horizon for signs of a green cloud. They were spared that horror, too.

"It's a nice day, don't you think?" Sansa remarked at one point.

"Sure," Courtney said. "Nice."

She was a lousy judge of distance but by her reckoning they had gone a couple of miles when the forest gave way to a stretch of farm country.

"I'm hungry," Sansa said.

"Makes two of us." Courtney noted. Her stomach had been growling for a good while.

Sansa pointed at a farmhouse off to the east. A dirt track wound across fields toward it. "I bet they have food."

"If anyone is home," Courtney said.

"Can we go? Please?"

"I'd rather stick to the road."

"Okay." Sansa didn't hide her disappointment.

They hiked on.

The talk of food made Courtney hungrier. She was imagining a plate heaped with eggs and home fries when Sansa let out a squeal of delight.

"Look!"

A junction appeared ahead. So did a building. A sign proclaimed it was *Abernathy's Market.*

Courtney stopped.

"What's an...," Sansa said, and pronounced the rest with uncertainty, ..."Abernathy?"

"A person's name."

"Never heard it before." Sansa grinned. "But there just has to be food at a market, right?"

"Maybe more than food."

"You mean trouble?"

Courtney nodded.

"I don't see anyone."

"Me either," Courtney said, Which meant nothing. Thanks to the oppressive overcast and tinted windows, the interior was cast in dark shadow. No lights were on.

An older pickup occupied a lone space in the parking lot.

Hefting the rifle, Sansa started forward.

"Wait," Courtney said.

"But I'm so hungry!"

"Me first. You follow but stay back, just in case."

"I bet there's candy," Sansa said dreamily. "I love candy."

Courtney went slowly, the shotgun level at her waist. In a field adjacent to the lot lay a body, the flesh mostly gone, the bones gleaming white. The owner? she wondered.

Half a dozen crows were perched on the roof, silent sentenils watching their approach. Courtney was almost to the lot when one squawked and they all took raucous wing.

Courtney looked up and down the side road. Not a vehicle, or any living thing, anywhere.

The pickup was close to the store. Dinged and dented, it had seen a lot of use.

Courtney was halfway across the lot when she was brought up short by movement inside. She couldn't tell if it was a person---a healthy one---or yet another of the living dead.

Taking a gamble, she called out, "Is someone in there? Show yourself! I promise I won't shoot!"

More movement suggested she had been heard. The front door---a wooden one, not pneumatic---opened.

And Courtney gasped.

Sally Ann emerged with a smile on her face and spread her arms as if in welcome. "Courts! Sansa!" she exclaimed.

Courtney lowered the shotgun. "You're alive!" she cried, so happy at finding her friend that she was fit to burst. She started forward, then stopped.

Sally Ann was doing a strange thing. While she continued to smile and her arms were still spread as if to embrace Courtney, Sally was blinking her eyes as fast as she could blink, over and over.

Puzzled, Courtney almost asked out loud if something was wrong. Then it hit her. There was. Her friend was blinking like that to warn her....but about what?

Courtney gave a nod to show she understood, and Sally's smile widened. "Come here and let me hug you."

Sally stayed where she was, and began to flick her right thumb to the right.

"Why is she doing that strange stuff?" Sansa called out.

A look of fear came over Sally.

Courtney was slow on the uptake. She should have caught on to the thumb flick. The reason resolved itself in the form of the biker Gramps, who strode around the corner of the market with a big semiautomatic held firmly in both hand---and pointed at Courtney's head.

"I can answer that for you, sweetie," Gramps said.

"The bitch is trying to warn her friend. Thanks for letting me know."

Courtney debated swinging the shotgun toward him and cutting loose but he must have guessed her intent.

"I wouldn't, girl," Gramps declared. "You shoot at me and your friend Sally gets clipped."

"Got that right!" said someone inside the market.

A rifle barrel jutted out the open door, fixed on Sally's back.

Courtney recognized Rufus' voice. If she fired at Gramps, Rufus would kill Sally. If she shot at Rufus, Gramps would blow her away.

"We've got you dead to rights, girl," Gramps gave voice to her fear. "Be smart and set that cannon down, nice and easy."

"Don't listen to him!" Sally Ann finally spoke.

"What other choice does she have, stupid?" Rufus snapped. Only part of his arm and shoulder were visible. "Or are you that eager to die?"

Gramps surprised Courtney by coming toward her. It made him an easier target, and made her easier to hit, too.

"Listen, we're not going to kill you if you don't make us," Gramps was saying. "Not even after all the crap you and your boyfriend pulled." He stopped and glanced down the road to the south. "Where is he, anyway?"

"Dead," Courtney said, the word an anchor in her heart.

"Shouldn't have turned on us," Gramps said. "He'd be alive now."

Sally Ann glared. "Don't act so noble."

"Noble, hell," Gramps said. "We would have kept

our word. Not laid a finger on any of you. Or snuffed you."

"Only until we reached the compound," Sally Ann said. "We were wise to your ruse."

"So you broke away first chance you got, and what did that get you?" Gramps said. A few lumps and pretty boy dead."

At the mention of 'lumps', Courtney looked at Sally Ann and noticed a bump on her temple and a bruise under her right eye. "Did one of them beat you?"

Gramps said, "She brought it on herself. Wouldn't listen."

"If it'd been up to me," Rufus threw in, "I'd slit her damn throat."

"Enough gab!" Gramps declared. He aimed his pistol. "Put the shotgun down or this gets ugly."

Courtney hesitated. To resist was suicidal. Yet part of her yearned to. It was Sansa who decided the issue.

"Don't do it, Courtney! I don't care if we do have to die!" the girl urged.

"You win," Courtney said. She slowly stooped and set the shotgun on the asphalt, then raised her arms.

"Courtney, no!" Sansa cried.

Sally Ann bowed her head. "She has no choice, little one."

"Take three steps back," Gramps commanded.

Smothering a wave of despair, Courtney obeyed.

"Don't try anything." Keeping his weapon on Courtney, Gramps advanced and snatched the shotgun off the ground.

Out of the store ambled Rufus, looking like a cat that ate three canaries. "Well, that was awful disappointing. I was hoping I'd get to shoot one of you bitches."

"What now?" Courtney said to Gramps. "The deal still holds? You'll take us to the compound and keep your hands to yourself."

"About that," Gramps said. "You might be of use finding the place. But as for our hands...." He grinned and licked his lips.

CHAPTER 20

It turned out that Gramps and Rufus had their bikes hidden behind the market.

"They've been waiting to see if any of their buddies showed up," Sally Ann explained after the two Claws ushered Courtney and Sansa and her into a storeroom and shut the door.

"Where did you disappear to after that mutate attacked?" Courtney was curious to learn.

"Gramps and Jenks tied me and left me in some brush while they and Rufus went back to look for the others."

"I shot Jenks," Courtney said.

Sansa tugged on Sally Ann's arm. "What about Willis?" she anxiously asked. "Where's he at?"

Sally frowned and gave the little girl's shoulder a squeeze. "I don't know. I'm sorry. When Gramps pulled me off the bike to tie me, he kicked Willis and Willis yipped and ran off into the woods."

"Oh," Sansa said bleakly. Averting her face, she moved to a corner and leaned her forehead against the wall and quietly began to cry.

"Poor kid," Sally Ann said.

Courtney was about to go comfort her when the door opened and Gramps filled the doorway. An energy drink was in one hand and a candy bar in the other. His pistol was wedged under his bulging gut. "All right. We're letting you out. But give us grief and we'll keep you in here until we're ready to leave."

"When will that be?" Courtney asked.

"A day or so," Gramps said. "We're giving our bros time to catch up." He scowled. "If any of them are still alive."

"Spike is," Courtney said. She didn't why she told him. Unless part of her was hoping that if they stayed there a good long while, Gramps and Rufus would let down their guard.

"That better be the truth," Gramps said.

"So help me," Courtney said.

"Then he'll show up eventually," Gramps predicted. "Where's Gaga?"

"Your mutt is out front, whining," Gramps said. "Be glad she's still breathing. Rufus is for carving her into pieces." He beckoned. "Move your asses."

Sally Ann followed him out.

Courtney went to Sansa, who was still weeping. "I'm sorry about Willis."

Sansa made a choking sound.

"Are you hungry? Let's go find something to eat."

Shaking her head, Sansa whispered, "I'd like to be alone. Please."

"Sure." Courtney was loathe to leave but she remembered the few times in her own life that she had cried. Misery didn't like company.

One of the bikers had lit a propane lantern and placed it on the front counter, relieving the gloom.

An odor permeated the market, from food that was spoiling. The smell would grow worse over the days ahead.

Rufus was contentedly chomping on jerky. Several cans of beer were next to him.

Gramps had helped himself to a bag of pretzels.

Sally Ann was waiting for Courtney. "What would you like? There are sandwiches in a cooler."

"I'd like a gun," Courtney said, and nodded at Granps and Rufus.

"We're lucky they're letting us live," Sally Ann said.

"Don't tell me you've given up?"

"Never." Sally Ann lowered her voice. "But we have to be smart. We may only get one chance."

"What are you two whispering about?"

Courtney and Sally Ann both gave a start.

Rufus had come up on them as silently as a slinking cat. "I asked you bitches a question."

"Nothing," Sally Ann said.

"Don't make me beat it out of you" Rufus took a bite of jerky and noisily chewed.

"We were talking about how we'd like to be free of you," Courtney admitted.

"Do tell?" Rufus said, and kicked her in the shin.

Pain exploded up Courtney's leg and she doubled over, barely able to keep her balance.

"Hey!" Sally Ann said.

Rufus punched her on the jaw.

Tottering back, Sally Ann clutched at a shelf for support and cans crashed to the floor.

"What the....!" Courtney got out, and Rufus slugged her, too. The jolt slammed her against the wall and pinpoints of light danced before her eyes.

"You dumbasses need to get a few things straight," Rufus growled, and drew back his fist. "Which of you wants to lose her teeth?"

Courtney cocked her knee to kick him where it would hurt a male the most but just then Gramps gave a holler.

"Rufus! You hear that?"

Courtney heard it, too. The metallic thrum of a motorcyle in the near distance.

"Guess who it is?" Gramps said cheerfully.

Rufus lowered his arm, spat on the floor in contempt, and headed up front.

"Are you all right?" Courtney asked Sally Ann, who was woozily shaking her head.

"The bastard can hit," Sally said.

"He'll get his."

Gramps and Rufus were at the front window, both grinning. The reason for their delight was the familiar figure of the skinny man with a Mohawk on the approaching bike.

"Good ol' Spike," Rufus declared.

"Now there are three of us bad boys," Gramps said.

Courtney nudged Sally Ann, put a finger to her lips, motioned, and together they hurried toward the storeroom.

Sansa was huddled in the corner, dabbing at her eyes. She bleated in surprise when Courtney scooped her up, and Courtney put a hand over her mouth to silence her. "Shh. We're getting out of here."

Courtney was half afraid the back door to the market would be locked. Fortune favored them. A hinge creaked but not loud enough to be heard up front.

The bikes belonging to Gramps and Rufus were parked close to the rear wall.

Courtney was tempted to knock them over in the hope of disabling them but the racket would draw Gramps and Rufus.

Sally Ann quietly closed the door.

A stand of trees about half an acre away caught Courtney's eye. "There!" she said, and ran.

"They'll know that's where we went," Sally Ann said, catching up.

"Can't be helped. It's the only cover."

"What's your plan? Sticks and stones against their guns?"

"Save your breath."

Sansa was keeping pace, her shorter legs pumping.

Plunging into the trees, Courtney skirted a thicket. In less than thirty feet, the stand ended at an open field.

There was no place to hide.

"They'll find us easy," Sally Ann said.

"Keep going."

They burst into the open space.

Materializing as if out of nowhere, Gaga was with them.

To their left a fair way was the road. To their right, nothing but more open field.

A bellow from the vicinity of the market warned them that the Claws were in pursuit.

Fury coursed through Courtney. Fury that the bikers wouldn't leave them be. Fury that the world had gone mad and there was nothing she could do about it. Fury that life would do this to her.

"Listen!" Sally Ann exclaimed.

It took a few seconds for the new sound to register. From overhead came the unmistakable sound of an aircraft.

A small plane, would be Courtney's guess. Despite herself, she slowed and scanned the thick cloud cover. The plane was low in the sky but she couldn't see it. The engine sputtered and coughed, then picked up again. Only for a bit. Again it sputtered.

"The pilot is having trouble and must be looking for a place to set down!" Sally Ann guessed.

As if that were a cue, out of the cloud dipped the aircraft, a yellow-and-green Piper Cub, Courtney believed they were called.

She stopped in astonishment. "How can it be flying?"

"Those bikes and some cars and trucks still work," Sally Ann reminded her.

The Piper Cub dropped lower. It flew the length of the open field, sputtering all the while, then banked and flew in a wide loop to come at the field from the far end.

"It's going to land!" Sally Ann cried.

The engine died and the Piper Cub shimmied. The pilot steadied it and descended smoothly, if abruptly. The front wheels touched and the plane bounced once, twice, three times, and then the wheels were down and the plane was slowing. It hit a hole or maybe a ditch and a wheel caught. Suddenly the aircraft spun crazily, the wings tilting.

For a moment Courtney thought it would flip over. But the pilot again regained control and the plane slid to a halt with the propeller pointed toward Courtney and her friends.

"They made it!" Sally Ann said.

"Good for them!" someone snarled.

Courtney spun.

Gramps, Rufus---and Spike---were only yards away and training guns on them.

"Miss me?" Spike said, and wagged his semiautomatic. He blew Courtney a kiss. "I sure missed you."

"The plane," Gramps said.

"What about it?" Spike said.

"We should see who it is."

"Duh."

"Maybe there's women!" Rufus said.

"We've got these two," Spike said, and winked at Courtney and Sally Ann.

"Why isn't anybody getting out?" Gramps wondered.

"Let's go see," Spike said. "Ladies first, if you don't mind, and even if you do."

"My kingdom for a gun," Sally Ann said.

"Huh?" Rufus said.

"A play on Shakespeare."

"A what on who?" Rufus said.

"God, you're dumb," Sally Ann said.

"Shut up, bitch!" Spike snapped. "Get walking!"

Courtney hoped the people in the plane were watching and would catch on that the Claws were trouble. The cockpit windows were tinted and there was no way of telling how many were inside.

"Smile, fellas," Spike said to his brothers in leather. "Pretend we're friendly as can be!"

"That's us," Rufus said, laughing.

Courtney desperately yearned to warn whoever was in there. She silently mouthed the words, "Help us!" a few times.

"This is close enough," Spike announced. He had lowered his pistol close to his leg. Rufus and Gramps had done the same with their guns.

"Hey, in there!" Gramps hollered, waving. "You folks okay?"

"Need any help?" Rufus said, and snickered.

The door on the pilot side of the Piper Cub opened. A black boot appeared, a cowboy boot, and slid to the ground. Than another, and legs in jeans. Around the door sauntered the man who wore them.

"Howdy," he said.

Courtney was thunderstruck. He was young, not much over twenty, if that, and so strikingly hot---at least to her---she felt something that she had never felt before; a strange sense of excitement.

He wore Western garb, including a black belt with a large silver buckle in the shape of a wolf's head, a checkered read and black shirt, and a dark blue coat of some kind that fell down to his ankles.

"Nice slicker you've got there, hoss," Gramps said.

The pilot's eyes were a piercing blue, his curly hair blond. He stood with his thumbs hooked in a second belt that crossed the first at an angle. His teeth, when he smiled at Courtney and Sally Ann and Sansa, were as perfect as those in a TV commercial.

"Ladies," he said.

His voice was low and deep, and to Courtney, seemed to strum a chord deep inside of her. "Hey," she blurted, feeling supremely stupid but unable to think of anything else. Her mind wasn't working right.

"Hi," Sally Ann said. She introduced herself and Courtney and Sansa. "And this is Gaga," she finished.

"Aren't you forgetting somebody?" Spike said.

"Get to you in a minute," the pilot said.

"How's that again, ace?" Spike said.

The pilot was staring at Courtney. She felt herself blushing and didn't understand why. "You need to.....," she was going to say 'be careful' but he spoke before she was done.

"Gar."

"Excuse me?" Courtney said.

"Gar," he said again. "My name."

Spike shouldered past Courtney and Sally Ann. "Gar, is it?" He held out his empty hand. "I'm Spike. Pleased to meet you."

Gar didn't shake.

"What's your problem, mister?" Spike said.

Gar ignored him. To Courtney he said, "You and Sally and the little one should move to the left a bit."

"Hey!" Spike said. "I'm talking to you, damn it."

It wasn't like Courtney to do what a complete stranger told her but she pulled Sally Ann and Sansa aside and waited breathlessly for the next development.

The Claws were glancing at one another in confusion. Finally Spike fixed his glare on Gar. "Where do you get off ignoring us? Treating us like dirt?"

"Who do you think you are?" Rufus chimed in.

Unruffled, Gar said calmly, "Saw you out the cockpit. Saw you chasing the ladies. Saw you point your weapons at them."

"You misunderstood, mister," Gramps said, smiling. "It's not like you think."

"Oh, it's plain as can be," Gar said.

"Enough of this," Rufus said. "Let's look in that plane and see if he's got anything we can use."

"Not going to happen," Gar said.

"Why the hell not?" Spike said.

For an answer, Gar used his right hand to slowly move his slicker aside.

Everyone stared.

CHAPTER 21

Courtney didn't know a lot about guns. Calibers, hollow points, muzzles-whatever, she'd never paid much attention. But she did know a revolver from a semiautomatic.

Gar wore a revolver the likes of which Courtney had never seen. The grips or handles looked to be made of pearl. Her mother owned pearl earrings, and they were the same color and texture. Oddly, they had a curve to them that brought to mind the beak of an eagle or a hawk. The revolver itself gleamed like silver. For some reason the term 'nickel-plated' popped into her head.

The holster was black leather, decorated with silver conchos, and cut low so that over half of the revolver was visible.

Gramps let out a whistle of appreciation. "Nice piece you have there, mister."

"Been in the family a good long while," Gar said quietly.

Spike was eyeing it as if it were made of diamonds. "Remington? Smith and Wesson?"

"Colt Lightning."

"I don't suppose you'd let me hold it?"

"Wasn't born yesterday," Gar said, "and we have business to tend to."

"We do?" Rufus said.

"Drop your guns and step back," Gar said.

"Be serious," Spike said.

"There's three of us, dummy," Rufus stated the obvious.

"Why the hostility?" Gramps said. "We haven't done anything to you."

"Ladies," the man called Gar said without turning his head to look at Courtney and her friends. "Am I right in how I read this? Would you rather be shed of these gents?"

"We sure as hell would," Sally Ann said.

"There you have it," Gar said to Spike. "So I'll say it just once more. Drop your hardware and you get to live."

Rufus snorted. "Listen to him!"

Gramps glanced at Spike. "He's too sure of himself. I say we back down."

"Too sure or too full?" Spike said. "And in case you've forgot, the Claws don't back down to anyone. Ever."

Gar said, "Mister, I've been using this Colt since I was knee-high to a calf. You may think you have the edge but you don't. I really don't want to kill you so do us both a favor and let it go."

"Killed a lot of people, have you?" Spike sneered.

"Two, before the world went to Hades" Gar said, and added, "In the line of duty."

"The service?" Gramps said.

"Deputy sheriff."

"I hate cops!" Rufus said. "A badge triggers me like nothing else!"

Spike shifted slightly, his hand still holding his pistol behind his leg. "Well, Deputy Dog, here's how it will be. *You* unbuckle *your* gunbelt and let it down easy, and *we'll* let *you* live."

"I've got a bad feeling about this," Gramps said.

Spike hissed at him. "What, the world comes to an end you turn into a wimp?"

"A man has to know when to fold his cards," Gramps said.

"Nothing doing. I want that pistol of his," Spike said.

"It's just a gun," Gramps said.

"I never saw one like it."

Rufus was eagerly shifting his weight from one foot to the other. "I just want to kill him."

"You get off on killing everything you can," Gramps said.

Rufus laughed. "It's like those potato chips. You can never get enough."

Gar said, "How about we have one of the girls count to three?"

"What?" Spike said.

"Why three?" Rufus said.

"Now you just hold on," Gramps said.

"Count to three, Courtney," Gar said.

Courtney couldn't say what made her do it. She started in without thinking. "One. Two. Three."

Spike swept his pistol up. Rufus started to raise his gun. Gramps was slower to react and jerked his big semiautomatic up.

Courtney caught it all out of the corner of her eye. She was watching Gar. She saw his hand flick, so quick that if she wasn't looking right at him, she would have missed it. Somehow, his pearl-handled Colt was up and out and booming in less than the blink of an eye. He fanned it three times, shots so swift, they were almost a single sound.

Gar's expression never changed. He was as calm and

relaxed as if he were turning on a TV. After the third shot, he held the Colt steady at his hip, ready to fire again should it be necessary.

It wasn't.

Spike, Rufus and Gramps lay sprawled in postures of violent death. Each had a hole in the middle of their forehead.

Spike and Rufus wore looks of dumb amazement.

"Sorry you had to see that, ladies," Gar said in his quiet way.

"I'm not," Sally Ann said. "I'd pay to see it again."

Gar stripped the dead Claws of their weapons and handed the rifle to Courtney and Gramps's pistol to Sally Ann. Spike's small pistol, Gar gave to Sansa.

Courtney arched an eyebrow. "She's a little young for that."

"Use to, she would be." Gar said in that drawl of his. "But now...." He motioned at the Claws. "I"ll show you how to shoot later on, little one," he told Sansa. "Right now we've got things to do."

"Taking over, are you?" Sally Ann said.

"Those shots might bring eaters," Gar replied.

"Is that what you call them?" Sally Ann said, and laughed. "We call them zombies."

"A rose is still a rose, right?" Gar said.

"Wow," Sally Ann said.

"What?" Courtney said. "What does a rose have to do with zombies?"

Neither answered her. Stepping to the Piper Cub, Gar opened the door. "How about a hand? I've got supplies we can use."

The cabin was smaller than Courtney imagined it would be, the space behind the pilot's seat crammed with packs and cases and whatnot. As Gar rummaged among them, she asked out of curiosity, "Is Gar your first or your last name?"

"My full handle is Garland Rhett Shannon," he said while opening a backpack.

"Handle?" Courtney said. "I never heard anyone call their name that."

"It's an old-time word," Gar said. "Folks still use it in the hills."

"Thank you for helping us," Courtney thought to say.

"Three damsels in distress," Gar said. "How could a gentleman not?"

"You talk strange," Courtney said. She liked it, though. She especially liked the slight twang to his voice.

"Where were you headed?" Sally Ann inquired.

"Canada, more or less," Gar said, taking a box of ammunition from the backpack and sliding it into a pocket on his slicker.

"More or less?" Sally Ann said.

Gar shrugged. "It didn't make much difference. I lost all my kin back to Arkansas. Figured Canada, there are less people than in the U.S., so fewer eaters. Plus I have a cousin up there somewhere."

"You sound so sad when you talk about that," Sansa said.

"I should be happy that my dad and mom and sis and brother are all gone?"

"I lost mine, too," Sansa said.

"Makes three of us," Courtney chimed in.

"Four," Sally Ann said.

"Sorry for all of us," Gar said sincerely. He held out

the backpack. "Can you tote this, pretty gal? It has a lot we'll need."

Grunting, Courtney hefted the pack, then realized what he had said. Hiding a smile, she swung the pack over her left shoulder. "Heavy."

"Cans and such," Gar said. "Now where are you ladies headed?"

"A survivalist compound," Courtney said. "We heard about it on the shortwave. Might be safer there."

"You reckon they'll take you in?"

Until that moment, Courtney hadn't give it much thought. She'd assumed that she and her friends would show up, knock on their door, and be admitted. People had to help each other, right?

"Courts," Sally Ann said, pointing. "We've got trouble."

A lone zombie---its clothes in tatters and splotched with red smears that must be dried blood---was approaching along the road from the north. It was a fast one, loping at a pace a human would be hard pressed to keep up. Hunched over, it raised its head from time to time as if it were sniffing.

"Maybe it won't notice us," Courtney hoped.

Gaga growled.

Instantly the zombie's head snapped around. Like a streak it vaulted a low ditch and sprinted toward the plane.

"If something ever goes right for us," Sally said, "I don't know if I could stand the shock."

Courtney sank to a knee and pressed the rifle to her shoulder. She'd need to wait until it was close enough to be certain.

"Let me, ladies," Gar said, moving to put himself

between them and the ghastly horror.

"We don't need babysitting," Sally Ann said.

"Perish forbid," Gar said.

The zombie rapidly closed. It was forty yards out. Then thirty. Hissing loudly, it bared its teeth.

"Ugly suckers," Gar said, and drew his revolver. This time he wasn't in any hurry. He casually drew and casually fired from the hip.

The top of the fast zombie's head exploded and their would-be slayer lurched, tottered, and fell.

"Piece of cake," Gar said, and grinned at Courtney. "Old family saying," he added, twirling his Colt into its holster.

"My dad had a saying," Courtney felt compelled to mention . "Where there's a will, there's a Hewitt."

"We'd best pick up the pace," Gar said. "We want to be long gone before they get here."

"They who?"

"There's a huge herd heading this way, coming from the south. I caught sight of them from the plane. Must be hundreds of the things."

"You didn't think to mention that sooner?" Sally Ann said.

CHAPTER 22

Laden with packs, they hurried to the market.

Courtney let Gar take the lead. It wasn't that he was a guy. He was a better shot, and better able to protect them.

"How about we use the bikes?" Sally Ann suggested. "It beats going on foot."

"Can you ride one?" Gar asked.

"Ride, as in shift gears?" Sally Ann shook her head.

Gar glanced at Courtney.

"Me neither."

"Then the bikes are out," Gar said. "I can, but I'm not about to leave any of you behind."

"You've only just met us," Sally Ann said. "You don't owe us anything."

"I owe myself."

Courtney wondered what he meant. She could feel herself being drawn to him, and it troubled her. The last time she felt anything like this was when she had a crush on the captain of the basketball team.

As they came around to the front, Gar caught sight of the pickup. "Does that run?"

"We haven't tried to start it," Sally Ann said.

Gar went to the truck and opened the driver's door. "No keys."

"Even if we had them, the odds are against it," Sally Ann said. "Most vehicles don't."

"Most isn't all."

They entered the market.

"Any space left in your packs," Gar said, "load up on canned goods and drinks."

Sally Ann chuckled. "Is it me or do you like giving orders?"

Gar made for the counter.

"I don't know about him," Sally Ann whispered to Courtney.

"I do,"

"How, pray tell? We've known the guy for all of ten minutes."

"Call it a hunch."

"Call it hormones, is more like it," Sally Ann said. "I've seen how you look at him."

"I look at him the same as I look at everybody."

Gar let out a whoop and came from behind the cash register jiggling a set of keys. "Look what I found in a drawer."

"How do we know one is a key to the pickup?" Sally Ann said.

"Were you born always looking at the bad side of things or have you worked at it?"

"Say what?" Sally Ann said.

Courtney laughed.

Gar went out and Courtney followed. He climbed in, smiled at her and crossed his fingers, and turned the keys. The starter ground but nothing happened.

"If at first...," Gar said.

It took six tries before the truck sputtered and belched a cloud of smoke and noisily rumbled to life.

Gar gave the dash a smack of delight. "Now we can travel in style."

"How is it fixed for gas?" Courtney brought up.

"Three quarters," Gar said. "This old model, I make it that the tank probably has around twenty gallons left, give or take a few. Let's say fifteen to eighteen gallons per mile. That gives us a range of three hundred to three hundred and sixty miles. Again, give or take."

"More than enough to reach the compound," Courtney said excitedly.

"Do you know anything more about the place? Anything at all?"

"Only what we told you. Why?"

"I just don't want to get there and have to shoot our way in."

"You'd do that?" Courtney said.

"I'll do whatever I have to to keep the three of you safe."

A warm sensation spread from Courtney's head to her toes. She was sure she blushed. To cover her reaction, she pretended to be interested in the sky.

Gar seemed to hesitate, then said, "You don't have a fella anywhere, do you?"

Taken aback, Courtney coughed. "Why do you want to know?"

"I've kind of taken a shine to you," Gar said, sounding surprised that he had.

"Courtney!" Sansa suddenly cried. "Zombies are coming!"

Courtney nearly jumped. She hadn't realized the girl was there.

Far off to the south, the road was jammed with lurching, shambling figures.

"Load up and we're out of here," Gar said.

Courtney lifted Gaga into the bed with the packs and supplies. Gaga whined and kept trying to climb back out so Courtney tied her to a ring on the side panel.

Once in the pickup, Courtney had Sansa sit on her lap. It was the only way they would all fit.

"Let our adventure begin!" Sally Ann declared as they wheeled from the lot.

Any hopes Courtney entertained of reaching the survivalist compound at Lake Bronson State Park quickly were soon dashed.

They hadn't gone more than a couple of miles when they came on a stretch of road that looked as if it had been melted. Something had caused the asphalt to bubble and rupture and clump for hundreds of yards. In spots, black fountains several feet high were frozen in place, as if the asphalt had solidified after being projected skyward.

Gar braked and got out.

So did Courtney and Sally Ann.

"I've never seen the like," Gar remarked.

"What could have caused this?" Courtney said.

Sally Ann bent and touched the tip of a finger to a black fountain.

"You might not want to....," Gar began.

Yipping in pain, Sally Ann jumped back and frantically rubbed the finger on his pants. "It burns!"

Courtney grabbed her friend's wrist and held it so they could see her hand. Tiny blisters had sprouted.

Tears welled in Sally Ann's eyes. "It hurts like hell!" She made as if to stick her finger her mouth but thought better of the idea.

Courtney turned to go to the pickup for a bottle of water but Gar had beat her there. He returned, unscrewing the cap. Without a word, he took Sally

Ann's hand and slid her finger into the bottle.

Immediately, relief washed over her and she smiled. "Oh! Thanks! That helps a lot."

"Keep your finger in there a while" Gar said when she went to pull it out. He nodded at the warped asphalt. "It's a cinch we can't drive over that. Would likely eat holes in our tires."

"So we go around," Courtney said.

The field was rutted and bumpy. Gar drove slowly but Courtney bounced so hard at one point, she cracked her head on the top of the cab. They were almost past the ruined asphalt when Sansa extended her arm and screamed.

A green mist, as high as the trees and stretching for a quarter of a mile, was crawling over a hill to the west.

"I've seen those before," Gar said.

"So have we," Courtney said. "If we're caught in one, we're dead."

"Or changed into a pus-covered nightmare," Sally Ann said.

"We should be able to outrun it," Gar said. Swerving to where the road resumed its normal course, he increased speed.

As Courtney watched, the green cloud roiled and shifted, tendrils sprouting like the arms on an octopus, thin whips that grew steadily larger.

"How does it *do* that?" Sally Ann marveled. "It's as if the thing is alive."

The speedometer was at seventy. Ahead, a straight stretch would enable them to leave the cloud well behind.

"Is it me," Sally Ann said, "or is that thing moving faster?"

Courtney's skin crawled. Her friend was right. The green cloud *was* moving faster. Not only that, it was angling down the hill on an intercept course. "No way."

"It won't catch us," Gar assured them.

"Courtney!" Sansa screamed.

Another cloud had appeared to the east. Bigger than the first, and spread over a wider front, it advanced toward the road, tendrils writhing and coiling.

"Two of them so close together?" Courtney said in dismay.

"For all we know they hunt in packs," Sally Ann said.

"They're clouds," Gar said, concentrating on his driving. "Not wolves."

"In the Twin Cities they were drawn to people as if hunting them." Sally Ann said. "Maybe they're some kind of nanite, programmed to assimilate us."

"What's a nanite?" Sansa asked.

"A tiny device," Sally Ann said. "So small, you can only see them through a microscope."

Courtney was more interested in the clouds. The new one was moving much faster than the first and had less ground to cover before it reached the road.

"It's almost like they're trying to catch us between them," Gar said.

Courtney thought so, too. Her arm around Sansa, she gripped the dash with her other hand, gripped it so tight, her knuckles were white.

The speedometer was past eighty, the fields and woods flying by.

"There's a curve ahead!" Sally Ann warned.

Gar braked hard, cutting their speed in half and bringing a squeal of protest from their tires.

"There! A town!" Sally Ann exclaimed.

A sign with the name and population flashed past so fast, Courtney couldn't read it.

Ahead stretched fifteen to twenty blocks of mostly businesses. Side streets were lined with typical suburban homes.

The inhabitants were either hiding indoors or roaming the streets seeking prey. At least seven zombies were prowling the main street alone.

A lot of the windows were shattered. Glass littered the sidewalks. About half the parking spaces were lined with cars that wouldn't start---or whose owners were no longer able to drive.

In almost the exact center of town, a multi-vehicle pileup blocked the road.

As best Courtney could tell, a semi had collided with three cars smack in the middle of an intersection.

Gar brought the pickup to a stop and in a burst of irritation, smacked the steering wheel. "We can't go around. There isn't room."

"Back up, then," Courtney said.

"Zombies," Sally Ann warned. "On the left."

"I'll take care of them," Gar said, and reached for the door handle.

"No! Wait!" Courtney practically shouted. She pointed.

An eerie green tentacle was slithering out of a side street behind them. Curling like an elephant's trunk, it writhed to either side and then rose into the air like a snake about to strike.

Over the tops of homes to the east, the green cloud became visible.

"It's here already!" Sally Ann marveled.

"It's moving so fast, we'll never outrun it!" Courtney

realized.

Gar shifted into reverse and tromped on the gas. Spinning the wheel, he slammed the pickup's tail gate into a pair of shambling horrors. The crunch of their bones was nearly drowned out by Gaga's yip of terror.

As if he were a race car driver, Gar whipped the pickup in close to the curb in front of a wide brick building "Come on!" he yelled, and sprang out.

Courtney didn't question why. For some reason she instinctively trusted him. She set Sansa down and quickly untied Gaga.

Gar had run to a door and was trying to twist the knob.

Above the door in bold letters was *ACME SHIPPING*.

"A warehouse?" Sally Ann said. "What good will this do?"

Gar didn't answer. He stepped back, drew his Colt, and shot the lock. There was a loud *spang* and he kicked the door and it flew open."Inside!" he hollered.

Tentacles were flowing up the main street.

Courtney followed Gar into the building, into a dark office with a couple of desks and chairs and a counter. Beyond, a door hung ajar.

Gar darted through it.

The warehouse ran the length of the block. Pallets laden with crates and boxes took up most of the space.

Gar sprinted toward the back. To the right were recessed stairs. He indicated they should descend.

Courtney noticed a window high on the wall.

Green vapor was drifting past.

"We're trapped," Sally Ann said accusingly as Gar joined them at the bottom.

Gar tried a door with *Maintenance* stenciled in block letters. It opened---into blackness. He took a small flashlight from his slicker and switched it on. "Stay close."

A narrow tunnel brought them to a room filled with tools and mops and a snow shovel. There was barely room for them to cram in.

As Gar has done with every other door, he closed this one.

"You think that will keep the cloud out?" Sally Ann said.

"Have you ever seen one go into a a building?" Gar said.

Sally Ann had to think about it. "No. But that doesn't mean they don't."

"I'm turning off the flashlight," Gar let them know.

Sansa's hand found Courtney's.

Gaga's nose pressed against her leg.

"Listen!" Sally Ann whispered.

From somewhere and everywhere came an eerie hissing. It rose and fell, growing slightly louder each time it rose.

"It's the cloud!" Sally Ann gasped. "Getting closer!"

So close, Courtney was sure it was coming down the tunnel toward them.

CHAPTER 23

Of all the horrific developments since the outbreak of World War III, the one that scared Courtney the most, the one she feared more than the ravenous dead and the pus-covered monstrosities, were the chemical clouds.

Everything about them was scary. How they looked like clouds yet crawled across the ground instead of floating through the sky. How, unlike true clouds, which were subject to the wind, chemical clouds could travel in any direction. And how, once the clouds enveloped a person or an animal, their victims were never seen again---or they emerged from the clouds changed.

So now, as the hissing continued to grow louder, Courtney experienced rising panic. An impulse came over her to throw the door open and run even though there was nowhere to run to. The only way out was through the tunnel. Still, she was on the verge of giving in when a small hand crept into hers, shocking her back to reality.

"I'm scared," Sansa whispered.

"I'm right here with you," Courtney said. The fact that Sansa looked up to her and relied on her for protection was like a splash of cold water in the face. She must be strong for the girl's sake, if not her own

Gar switched off the flashlight.

In the sudden and total dark, Sansa wrapped both of

her arms around Courtney and trembled in fear.

"Why did you do that?" Sally Ann whispered.

"Shhhh," Gar said.

The hissing seemed to fill the storage room.

Gaga whimpered.

Courtney bit her bottom lip to keep from screaming. She was facing the door, and she thought she detected a faint green tinge at the bottom. She imagined green mist seeping in, and imagined the consequences should they breathe it.

Courtney blinked, and the green along the door was gone. She realized it had never been there to begin with.

Sansa was rigid with fear. "I don't want to die!"

"You're not about to, girl," Gar said. "Use your ears."

Courtney used hers.

The hissing sound was fading. The cloud, or the part of it that had slithered into the tunnel, was departing.

"Can we be this lucky?" Sally Ann said.

Pale light bathed them as Gar turned on the flashlight. Pressing an ear to the door, he listened, then said, "I think it's gone."

"Let's wait a while to be sure," Sally Ann said.

"It will be dark out soon," Gar said. "Better if we're gone by then."

"Why not hole up?" Sally Ann said. "Find a place with beds and spend the night?"

"In a town overrun with eaters?"

"I'm exhausted," Sally Ann said. "I've give anything for a good night's sleep."

"Wouldn't we all?" Courtney said. "But staying alive comes first."

"Great minds," Gar said, smiling at her.

Courtney grew warm again. It bothered her, how she reacted to him. As if she had no control over her feelings.

Gar had gone on. "The three of you wait here while I make sure the coast is clear."

"No way," Sally Ann said.

Courtney nodded. "We stick together no matter what."

"Your call," Gar said. He eased the door open a crack and peered out. "Looks safe." He breathed deeply a few times. "The air, too."

"We hope," Sally Ann said.

As a precaution, Courtney held her breath until they reached the top of the stairs. The warehouse appeared empty of life.

Once again Gar took the lead, moving from pallet to pallet in a crouch, his hand on his pearl-handled pistol.

Courtney hoped she wouldn't need to use the shotgun. One blast would bring every zombie around.

The office door was ajar yet Courtney distinctly remembered Gar closing it. Gar did, too, because he inched the door outward and checked before stepping through.

The front door was open, as well.

They crept to the window and parted the blinds.

Their pickup was where they had left it.

Only now the street around it was filled with zombies.

"There must be fifty or more!" Sally Ann exclaimed.

"A lot to fight our way through," Courtney said. More were approaching every second.

"Even if we did," Gar said, "the road is still blocked."

"We need another vehicle," Sally Ann said.

"And give up our supplies?" Courtney said.

Gar was craning his neck to see in all directions. "No sign of the green cloud. But it could come back." He frowned. "As much as I hate to say it, we might have to forget about the pickup." He turned. "Come on."

Sansa's hand glued itself to Courtney's.

"How are you holding up?" Courtney asked.

"I'm good so long as I'm with you."

An EXIT sign hung over a metal door at the rear of the warehouse. Gar pressed on the handle but the door didn't budge. He pushed harder, with no result. "Stay here," he said, and jogged toward the office.

"He sure likes to give orders," Sally Ann said.

"He's helping us," Courtney defended him. "We should be grateful."

"You like him, don't you?"

"Now's hardly the time."

"I'm not getting on your case or anything."

"Good."

"We'll always be besties,"Sally Ann said. "We can say anything to each other and no hard feelings, right?"

"In that case," Courtney said. "You're down all the time. It's not like you."

"Yeah, I admit it," Sally Ann said. "My dad dying. Then we lost Billy." She bowed her head in sorrow. "Throw in the end of the world, and is it any wonder?"

"We reach the compound, we'll be safe."

"You hope. We could get there and find out it's run by a bunch of loonies."

"There you go again."

"Just saying."

"We don't have to stay there if we don't like it," Courtney said. "We'll go our own way."

"If they'll let us."

Gar came running back with a key chain. He tried three keys before one worked. Putting a finger to his lips, he pushed as gently and quietly as he could. Even so, there was a scraping noise. He peered out. "The coast looks clear. But stay close together."

Not that Courtney needed reminding.

An empty street separated the warehosue from a residential area. Homes lined the other side. Except for the absence of life---no people, no dogs or cats or anything---the neighborhood seemed perfectly ordinary.

Gar hastened across and entered a trimmed yard, circling to pass between two houses.

Courtney's nerves jangled at being in the open in a town full of eaters. She liked that word better than zombies. The sole purpose of the creatures was to eat the living.

The next street was also peaceful.

To their left a car was parked at the curb. Gar didn't bother with it. Nor with a hybrid across from them. He was interested in an older car, a sleek green model, near the end of the block.

Staying alert, dreading the worst, Courtney glanced every which way. She saw movement in the second story window of a house but couldn't tell who, or what, it was.

"My grandpa had one of these," Gar said as he reached for the driver's door. "It's a Mustang."

Courtney vaguely remembered something about a movie with a famous scene involving a Mustang---her dad liked the movie a lot.

Gar poked his head in. "No key. To be expected, I

reckon."

The car was parked in front of a house with a porch and shutters.

"Whoever owns it must live there," Gar guessed. "I'll go have a look."

"Not alone you won't," Courtney said.

Gar grinned and winked at her. "Yes, ma'am."

Courtney checked in both directions, and stiffened.

The next block over, eaters had appeared. Five of them, shuffling and lurching.

"Get down!" Courtney whispered, and flattened, pulling Sansa down with her.

An eater turned toward them, and slowed.

Courtney was ready to scoop Sansa up and run for the house but the creature sniffed and grunted and trailed after the others.

The next moment, Gar was up and dashing to the porch. He tried the doorknob and gave them a thumb's up.

Only when all of them were safely inside did Courtney relax. For all of thirty seconds.

That was when Sansa screamed.

CHAPTER 24

To one side was an open closet for coats and jackets, half full. To the other, a broad parlor filled with furniture.

In the middle of the room lay a blue coiled fabric rug.

In the middle of the rug squatted an abomination.

Once, it had been a human being, a person so obese, they used a motorized cart to get around, even in their own home. The cart was on its side near the widescreen TV.

The woman who formerly relied on the cart now resembled a gigantic toad, her great moon face pasty with peeling flesh, her dead eyes as white as paper, her blubbery lips agape, exposing yellow teeth. Her thick arms were propped like forelegs, her real legs splayed to either side.

The woman wore a white robe decorated with pink bunnies. It had come loose, so that more of the woman spilled out.

The woman---the *thing*---fixed her white eyes on them, and belched.

Sansa screamed a second time.

Gar moved to put himself between them and the creature. He was unprepared for the sudden rush of speed the thing put on. Pumping her stout arms and stouter legs, and gnashing her yellow teeth, the thing hurtled at them.

Gar resorted to his pearl-handled pistol. He didn't

quite have it out when the woman slammed into him like an express train and sent him flying. His head struck the wall with a loud thud and he fell in a heap.

Sally Ann attempted to level her rifle but like Gar she was too slow. The creature lowered its head and rammed into her like a mad bull, and the impact sent Sally Ann tumbling.

That left Sansa, and Courtney.

Seizing the girl's arm, Courtney flew toward stairs to the second floor. She had no time to cut loose with the shotgun. She reached the stairs and bounded up them, past a stair lift.

The toad-woman never slowed. She didn't bother with the lift. She scrambled up the stairs with inhuman speed and agility.

Courtney heard the clack of teeth, and glanced down. The thing had missed biting her ankle by inches.

Practically lifting Sansa, Courtney ran faster. At the landing she spun and sought to kick their pursuer in the head but the woman twisted aside.

Courtney raced along a hallway. The first door she came to, she flung it open, pushed Sansa in and followed, and slammed the door after them. Pressing her shoulder to it, she braced her legs.

A resounding crash shook the door so violently, Courtney was knocked back. She pressed her entire body against it, hoping against hope it would hold.

Another impact popped the top hinge. A third caused the entire door to jump in the jamb.

The next would bring it crashing down, taking Courtney with it.

Courtney backpedaled, bringing the shotgun to bear. A round was already in the chamber. She fired just as another tremendous blow swept the door inward---on top of her.

Courtney fired an instant before the door struck. Wood exploded and splintered and then her arms were hit a jarring blow that knocked the shotgun from her grasp and the door crashed against her chest. She fell, the door on top of her, and heard Sansa shriek her name.

She tried to pushed the door, and couldn't. Scrabbling sounds told her the creature was slithering on top of it.

Straining for all she was worth, Courtney pushed but couldn't lift the door a fraction. She peered over the edge to see how close the creature was, and gasped.

That great moon face reared above hers. An inhuman smile lit the abomination's features. Those dead eyes seemed to gleam with life---or was it hunger?

The creature snapped at Courtney's fingers. She jerked them away barely in time. Those yellow teeth swooped lower, narrowly missing Courtney's cheek.

Courtney pushed, with no effect.

The woman's thick fingers curled into view, spread like claws, and descended toward Courtney's throat.

Courtney nearly screamed.

Those blubbery gums spread wider and the woman bit at her forehead and her eyes.

For heartbeats that were an eternity, Courtney stared her own death in the literal face. Then the woman's left cheek burst in a spray of putrid flesh and gore and bone.

Simultaneously, the boom of a shot shook the room.

The creature's eyelids fluttered and its dead white eyes rolled up into its head and its huge bulk went limp.

A leg and a boot gave the thing a shove and it rolled

off the door. The door itself was flung aside, and Gar bent and helped Courtney off the floor.

"Did she bite you?" Gar anxiously asked.

Courtney was still in shock, and couldn't get her vocal chords to word.

"Did she bite you?" Gar repeated, looking her over.

"No," Courtney got out.

"Thank God," Gar said, and hugged her.

Surprise replaced the shock, rendering Courtney speechless. Surprise that he cared so much. Surprise, too, that she liked that he cared.

"I got up here as quick as I could," Gar was explaining. Suddenly he stepped back and coughed. "Sorry. Didn't meant to touch you without your say-so."

"It's fine," Courtney said, her own throat oddly tight.

Sansa and Gaga ran to Courtney's side, the girl, as usual, wrapping her arms around Courtney's leg.

"I was so scared!"

"Makes two of us," Courtney admitted.

"We'd best find the keys to the Mustang," Gar said, and went out.

Sansa was staring at the mound of flesh that had once been a woman. "She was a monster, wasn't she?"

Courtney nodded, then realized something. "Where's Sally Ann?"

"Don't know."

They hurried downstairs.

Sally Ann was seated on the floor, doubled over, both arms across her chest.

"Sal?"

Her voice laced with pain, Sally Ann said, "I wanted to come help but I can barely move."

"It's all right," Courtney assured her.

"I think that bitch....",″ Sally Ann caught herself and glanced at Sansa. "I think a rib is cracked. Maybe two. It hurts just to breathe."

"Rest, then," Courtney advised. "I'll look for painkillers."

The bathroom seemed their best bet. The cabinet was crammed with medicine, both over the counter and prescription. One of the bottles Courtney recognized as being for diabetes. Another was a mood enhancer, the same kind an aunt of hers took for chronic depression. She also found three different kinds of pain relievers.

Sally Ann hadn't moved.

"Which do you want?" Courtney asked, holding them out.

Sally Ann tapped one.

"I'll get water."

The kitchen smelled of food gone bad, and worse. A partially eaten cat lay in a corner near a litter box. The back door was ajar a fraction, and Courtney closed it. As she did, she saw body parts strewn about the lawn, an arm here, a leg there, elsewhere the head---a man's---and part of a neck. The torso was on its belly, what hadn't been consumed.

Courtney tried the sink, worried the tap wouldn't work. The water trickled enough to fill a glass.

Sally Ann was waiting, a couple of capsules in her hand. She popped them into her mouth, and gulped the water. "Better work fast," she muttered.

Gar came down the stairs, twirling a key ring on a finger. "Guess what was on a nightstand?"

"We can get out of here!" Courtney said.

"When you start that car up," Sally Ann said through clenched teeth, "you'll have every zombie within blocks down on us."

"We'll be gone before they can surround us in big enough numbers," Gar predicted. He went to the front window and looked out. "Damn."

Courtney joined him.

Eaters were shuffling about in the street near the Mustang.

"I count eight," Gar said.

Several more tottering around a house, including a man with only one arm.

"They heard the ruckus," Gar said.

"But they're not sure where it came from," Courtney said.

Gar shrugged. "Can't be helped. Once I'm in the car, I'll lead them off. Go a few blocks and circle back. Be ready to run when I show up."

"It would be safer to wait until all of them drift elsewhere," Courtney suggested.

Gar went to respond but a loud series of thumps caused them both to turn.

The toad woman wasn't dead. She was coming down the stairs.

Half her cheek and part of her jaw was missing, and her hideous bulk shook as if she were having a seizure. Yet for all that, the woman pumped her thick arms and dragged her legs, intent on reaching them so she could sink her yellow teeth into their bodies.

"What does it take to kill that thing?" Courtney said.

"Let's find out," Gar replied. Darting to the fireplace, he snatched a brass poker from a rack.

The dead woman reached the bottom of the stairs--

-and Gar was waiting. Raising the poker in both hands, he speared the tip into the top of her head.

The woman uttered an inhuman screech, and incredibly, kept crawling toward Courtney and Sansa.

Gaga fearfully backed away.

Courtney raised her shotgun but thought better of using it. The blast might draw others.

Gar, still holding onto the poker, gave it a violent wrench.

Stiffening, the toad-woman commenced to thrash like a fish on a hook. She flung her arms, she bucked.

Gar pressed down on the poker with all his weight.

Abruptly, the thrashing ended and the creature sagged.

"Damn," Gar said.

"Finally!" Sally Ann exclaimed.

Gar left the poker jutting from the woman's head and went to the front window and peered out. "As many as before, if not a few more."

"We should wait, I tell you," Courtney insisted.

"Be ready," Gar said, and hastened down the hall.

"He sure isn't one for taking advice," Sally Ann said.

"We have no cause to complain," Courtney said.

"Says the girl who thinks he's hot," Sally Ann teased.

Courtney could see the kitchen from where she stood, and saw Gar slip out the back door. Anxious for his safety, she moved to the blinds.

"He'll have to draw them away to reach the Mustang," Sally Ann said.

The question of how he would do it was answered when loud banging, as of metal on metal, broke out from further down the street. The eaters jerked their heads up and shambled toward the noise. All except one that was staring fixedly at the sky.

The banging stopped but the zombies didn't and no sooner were they out of sight than Gar sprinted around the corner of the house and made for the Mustang.

The zombie staring at the sky went on doing so as if mesmerized.

Gar flung the Mustang's door open and slid in. Inserting the key, he twisted, then grinned toward the house when the engine roared to life.

"He lured most them off so we should go," Sally Ann said, moving to the front door.

Courtney hesitated. She recalled Gar saying something about drawing them off in the car. But Sal was right. All of the creatures except that sky-gazer were gone. She grabbed Sansa by the hand and told Gaga to come.

They were outside and starting across the lawn when the Mustang gave another roar---and shot down the street, swiftly accelerating. At the intersection it turned left, its tires screeching.

"He didn't even look our way!" Sally Ann said.

"Is he leaving us?" Sansa asked.

"He'd never do that," Courtney said. Although, given how little she knew about him and how short a time they had been acquainted, how she could be so sure was beyond her.

The zombie looking at the sky found something new to interest him---them.

And up the street a ways, two more eaters were tottering in their direction.

"Back inside," Sally Ann said.

Courtney wheeled, and froze.

Unnoticed, yet another of the walking corpses had

come around the far corner of the house and was now between them and the front door.

"He's mine," Sally Ann said, drawing her knife. "We have to do it quietly."

The new zombie was a big one. Not obese, like the woman inside, but in life he had stood inches over six feet in height and weighed somewhere close to two hundred and fifty pounds. His thick fingers were caked with blood and gore.

"I should shoot him," Courtney cautioned. "He's too big."

"And bring the rest back down on us?" Shaking her head, Sally Ann warily circled.

To keep the creature distracted, Courtney smacked her hand against her shotgun.

It worked. Or seemed to. The big brute fixed its dead white eyes on her.

Quickly sidling closer, Sally Ann raised her knife to strike.

Two things happened simultaneously.

The big zombie flicked out an arm and seized Sally Ann by the wrist.

And a hand that stank to high heaven and was pasty with rotting flesh clamped onto Courtney's shoulder from behind.

Sansa screamed.

Courtney barely heard her. She was whirling toward the zombie that had hold of her. It was the sky gazer. He had reached her faster than she had imagined he could.

Courtney tried to shove him off but his fingers were dug deep. She slammed the shotgun against his side but it did no good.

The thing tried to bite her neck.

Sansa screamed a second time.

Out of the corner of her eye, Courtney glimpsed Sally Ann on the ground, desperately trying to keep the big zombie from getting at her.

Courtney drove her knee at the groin of the thing that had hold of her. It, too, had no effect.

Courtney rammed the shotgun's muzzle into the creature's throat. The rotting flesh split and out oozed ugly fluids and an awful stench.

Courtney squeezed the trigger.

At the blast, the zombie's neck and most of the back of its head showered the lawn.

Courtney had never fired the shotgun one-handed before. The recoil was greater than she anticipated. The barrel whipped up and struck her on the chin, knocking her back and causing fireflies to dance before her eyes.

Her vision cleared and she saw that two more were almost on top of them. Pumping the shotgun, she shot one in the chest, pumped again, and shot the other one in the face.

She turned to see how Sally Ann was faring---and a hand like iron seized her by the ankle.

The big zombie was holding Sally Ann down with one huge hand pressed to her chest, and had now reached over and grabbed Courtney with its other huge hand.

Courtney pointed the shotgun but didn't shoot. She might hit Sally Ann.

Sansa overcome her fear and began kicking the big zombie in the back of its legs, again and again. She might as well have been a flea trying to hurt a gorilla.

Courtney went to swing the shotgun like a baseball bat but her leg was brutally yanked out from under her. She came down hard on her back, and the zombie pressed his hand to her chest.

Now both she and Sally Ann were pinned.

The zombie spread its mouth and bent to bite.

Twisting her face aside, Courtney saved herself. Wet drops spattered her neck, and she realized the big zombie was drooling. She heaved and kicked, as Sally Ann was doing, but the zombie was stronger than both of them, combined.

Then Courtney heard the roar of an engine. A horn blared and the zombie looked up as the Mustang slewed to a stop in the middle of the lawn. Out sprang Gar. A flick of his hand and his old Colt was out and pointed. He fired once, from the hip as he usually did, and the big zombie's forehead sprouted a hole.

In slow motion, the big eater melted to the ground.

Pushing out from under its arm, Courtney stood and helped Sally Ann up.

Gar had turned toward several more eaters coming around the next block. "Get in, ladies!"

Courtney didn't need to be told twice. She pulled the passenger front seat forward so Sansa and Sally Ann could climb in, then claimed the front seat for herself. Gaga tried to jump onto her lap but Courtney shifted the dog to the back seat.

Gar wasted no time in putting the pedal to the metal. On reaching the street he peeled out as if at a stock car race. He took the corner with the tires squealing.

"Can't leave you gals alone for a minute, can I?" he joked.

"Didn't expect you to take off," Sally Ann said.

"Told you I would." Gar looked over at Courtney. "You okay?"

Courtney nodded.

"I'm okay too," Sally Ann said. "Not that anyone asked."

"You're safe now," Gar said.

Sally Ann bent toward them, her eyes brimming with tears. "None of us will ever be safe again. Even at this compound we're going to." She added, "If we even reach it."

"Don't let all this get you down," Courtney said. It was Sally Ann who had bolstered her own spirits right after everything fell apart, and she was returning the favor.

"It's wearing on me, Courts," Sally Ann said softly.

"You're the one who said we can't give up hope."

"Maybe I was wrong."

"Like blazes you were," Gar interjected. "Hope is all we've got. Well, that and each other. We stick together and we'll make it."

Courtney resisted an urge to reach over and squeeze his hand.

"I'm not saying it will be a piece of cake," Gar said. "We're bound to run into more of those things, and who knows what else."

"God help us," Sally Ann said.

CHAPTER 25

Courtney was glad to be on the road again. Glad to be shed of the town whose name she still didn't know, glad to be snug and warm in the Mustang. The purr of the motor was a tonic for her frayed nerves. It reminded her of days past, days not so long ago when the world was peaceful and orderly and the worst thing she had to worry about was which clothes to wear to school. God, she'd had it easy, and had no clue.

Sansa had fallen asleep, cuddled against Gaga.

Sally Ann, though, was staring out the window, her face creased in worry.

"What?" Courtney said.

"Eh?"

"You look like that time the Spellman kid asked you out on a date. You were afraid what everyone would think since he was a nerd."

"Was I ever that ridiculous?" Sally Ann said, more to herself than to Courtney. "I didn't have a clue."

"OMG. I was just thinking the exact same thing," Courtney said. She turned to Gar. "How about you?"

His attention was fixed on the road. "How about me what?"

"Has the end of the world made you think twice about your life before it all went to hell?"

"No."

"Really?" Courtney found it hard to believe.

"I'm the same now as I was before the missiles hit,"

Gar said. "Only now I don't have to hold back."

"Hold back how?"

Taking his right hand off the steering wheel, Gar patted his pearl-handled Colt. "This."

"I don't get you."

"I can kill when I have to. With no worries about the law or anything."

Courtney let that sink in. "Wait. You like to kill?"

"Of course not," Gar said. "But if I have to, like back when my plane came down and I saved your hash, I can do what needs doing without having to worry about being tossed in jail or going on trial or any of that."

"What a strange way to look at it," Courtney said.

"Before all this happened," Gar said, "did anyone ever try to kill you?"

"Be serious."

"Rape you?"

"God, no."

"Beat you up?"

"I was in a fight once with another girl, in middle school. Not that it was much of a fight. Some slaps. Some name calling. That was all."

"So you've pretty much lived your whole life in a bubble."

"If you mean there wasn't much violence in my life, then yeah, sure. Thank goodness."

"Not everyone is so lucky," Gar said. "Not everyone lives in a nice, neat world where mommy and daddy look after their every need until they're old enough to fend for themselves."

"Isn't that how it is with most people? In our country, anyway. Most everyone always has enough food on the table and clothes to wear and no one tries to hurt them or put them under the ground."

"Used to be, it was," Gar said. "But then the politicians screwed things up so badly, we had homeless and addicts all over the place."

"I'd see them on the news a lot," Courtney said, feeling foolish saying it.

"From the safety of your bubble," Gar said.

"I don't see what that has to do with you being happy you can kill without ending up in prison."

"Only when I have to," Gar said. "Look, before all of this...," and he gestured at the outside world, "people had no choice but to let themselves be pushed around. If you hit someone, even in self-defense, you could end up in trouble with the law, or sued. You had to be careful to toe the lines of the bubble, or else." He smiled. "That's no longer the case."

"Who thinks of such a thing?" Courtney said.

"You better start," Gar said. "You and your friend, both. Those fellas, those bikers who caught you, from what you'd told me, they would have done you in, eventually. All because you wouldn't stand up for yourself and do what needed doing before it reached the point it did."

In the back seat Sally Ann said, "We tried, sort of."

"Keep trying," Gar said. "And get better at it. Or you won't survive the Apocalypse."

Courtney frowned. "I'm not going to become a killer just because the world has turned into one giant bloodbath."

For over an hour they drove in silence. The road remained clear of obstructions. Twice they came on hamlets which Gar skirted, taking side roads. He did the same to avoid Detroit Lakes. Strangely, they didn't see a single zombie.

Courtney was beginning to think that the worst might be behind them when they rounded a curve and up ahead, smack in the middle of the road, a giant stake had been imbedded.

With someone impaled on it.

Gar slammed on the brakes so hard, Courtney thrust her hand against the dashboard to keep from being flung against it.

Sally Ann did the same thing with the driver's seat, while Sansa woke up with a start and glanced fearfully around.

"What is it? What's wrong?"

"You don't want to see, little one," Sally Ann said. "Look away."

Courtney wished she could.

The stake was ten feet high and half as big around as a telephone pole. It had been driven through solid asphalt. The top end was sharpened to a point, and someone had forced a naked woman down onto the pole so that it drove up through her body and came out just below her chin.

Courtney's gut churned. In her new life of horrors, this was one of the most horrific. The victim was young, not much older than she was, and judging by the expression of terror and agony on woman's face, had died a hideous death.

"Who would do such a thing?" Sally Ann bleated.

"Is it some kind of warning?" Courtney wondered.

"The important question," Gar said, "is are they still around?"

Past the stake, the road ran through a cluster of houses.

"I don't see anyone," Sally Ann said.

Neither did Courtney. "Maybe everyone has left."

Gar pointed. "There's one who didn't."

A second stake, similar to the first, had been imbedded toward the middle of the hamlet. This time it was a naked man, middle-aged, his belly sagging, the sharp end of the stake jutting from his open mouth.

"What an awful way to go," Sally Ann said.

"It would have taken four or five men to lift him that high," Gar said.

"A sacrifice, you think?" Sally Ann said.

"In this day and age?" Courtney said.

"We should go around this place," Sally Ann suggested.

"Would that we could," Gar said. "You see any side roads?"

There were none, Courtney realized.

Gar slowly eased the Mustang around the first stake.

Courtney clenched her hands tight. She glanced right, left, right, left. Whoever the people were who could do such a thing....nothing was beyond them.

They came to the second stake. Again Gar went around, barely missing a ditch.

"Keep your head down," Sally Ann said to Sansa, who was trying to look out.

"Maybe we're in luck," Gar said. "Maybe no one is around."

They came abreast of the last house and Courtney let out a breath of relief.

A curve appeared, screened by trees.

Gar gained speed. They were into the curve when once again he slammed on the brakes.

The road was blocked. A pair of telephone poles had

been placed across it, the severed wires still attached. There was no way to go around because of trees.

"A trap, maybe!" Sally Ann said.

Courtney cradled her shotgun but no threats appeared.

The Mustang sat idling, Gar peering out the windshield.

"We should find another way" Sally Ann said.

Nodding, Gar shifted in his seat. "I'll back up." He looked out the rear window. "Oh, hell."

Courtney turned, and thought she was seeing things. Her brain refused to accept the reality. It simply could not be.

Yet it was.

Lumbering toward them, blocking their retreat, was a mutated monster, in every sense of the word. Easily twelve feet tall, with shoulders as wide as a bull's and an elephantine bulk, it was an abomination of Nature. Not that Nature had anything to do with its creation. Chemical and biological weapons were to blame, or more likely, a combination of the two.

Its head was misshapen, a repulsive pale moon cratered with oozing sores. The rest of its skin---it was entirely naked---was pitted and discolored. Most of its hair had fallen out. Insanity, and ferocity, gleamed in its wide eyes.

In its right hand it held a gigantic club.

Which it raised, and attacked.

"Get us out of here!" Sally Ann shouted.

Gar spun the wheel and buried the gas pedal, trying to swerve around the monster. But there wasn't room. The rear corner of their car struck the creature's leg. It was like striking a wall.

The club---it looked to be part of a utility pole---smashed onto the trunk with such force, it buckled the metal.

Gaga let out a howl of terror.

Courtney frantically began rolling down her window to get a clear shot.

Roaring like a beast, the mutation stooped and hooked a bulging forearm under the back of their car.

Incredulous, Courtney felt the Mustang rise. The thing was lifting the rear end into the air.

At the same time, it swung its club at the back window.

"Get down!" Sally Ann bawled, flinging herself at Sansa.

Glass burst in a shower of shards.

Gar reached for his door handle. "I'll get out and try to stop it!"

By then Courtney had her window down. "No! Let me!" She shoved the upper half of her body out.

Like King Kong over that train, the abomination loomed over the Mustang. Its mad eyes found her.

Courtney started to bring the shotgun to bear, only to have it stop short. She glanced down to discover the sling had caught on the lock.

"Look out!" Gar bellowed.

Courtney jerked back just as the gigantic club swished past her face. Unhooking the sling, she leveled the shotgun at the thing's broad chest.

The buckshot mangled flesh and sprayed gore. It left a hole Courtney could sink her fist into.

All the monster did was take a half-step back, grunt, and return to the attack---while still holding the Mustang off the ground.

Gar tramped on the gas but they couldn't break free.

Courtney pumped another round into the chamber. This time she pointed the muzzle at that great moon face. At those fierce eyes. Her finger was tightening on the trigger when a tremendous blow to her shoulder slammed her against the car. Her vision swam, her awareness dimmed.

Suddenly weak, struggling to retain her grip on the shotgun, she sagged against the door.

"It hit her!" Sansa shrieked.

Courtney heard as if through a great tunnel. The world had become a confusion of colors and sounds. She couldn't focus. Dimly, she felt a jolt to her body as the Mustang was slammed to the ground.

The creature had let go.

Sansa yelled something.

Sally Ann shouted something.

Courtney blinked, and raised her head, and the monster was right there beside her, its fingers splaying wide. Too late, she realized it was reaching for her. She tried to pull away but couldn't. Her body wouldn't do as she wanted.

She felt her hair gripped, felt her head wrenched up.

Her sight cleared, and her belly did flip-flops.

She was staring the thing in the face.

The creature had bent down so they were nose-to-nose. Sniffling loudly, it appeared to be studying her.

Why, Courtney couldn't say. Why it didn't just kill her, she would never know. She attempted to pull loose and the creature growled and shook her in annoyance. It was a wonder her spine didn't break.

Strangely, Courtney wasn't scared. She was mad more than anything, mad that this monstrosity had its hand on her, mad that she was helpless in its grasp, mad that it was undoubtedly going to kill her and there was absolutely nothing she could do.

Or was there? She sought to raise the shotgun but her arm was pinned.

In her anger, she snarled, "Let go of me, you bastard!"

The creature rumbled deep in its chest.

"Let go!" Courtney screamed.

New rage fueled the monster's features. It roared, and struck her head against the car.

The pain was overwhelming.

So was the wave of blackness that descended with startling swiftness. Again Courtney struggled, desperate to stay alert, to stay alive. Sansa was screaming and Gar yelled for someone to stay down, and there was the boom of a shot, followed by several more.

The pressure in Courtney's hair lessened. She tried to say Gar's name as the blackness enclosed her like a shroud.

CHAPTER 26

The first thing Courtney became aware of was a strange smell. It reminded her of the times her mother made her clean the kitchen, and the spray she used on the counters. A chemical smell she never liked.

She felt sluggish and disoriented. Her brain wasn't working right. She tried to remember where she was and suddenly a horrible image filled her head.

With a gasp, Courtney regained her senses. She opened her eyes and tried to sit up, and had to sink back back. Pain exploded, threatening to plunge her back into the darkness.

A gentle hand on her shoulder steadied her.

"Careful there, missy. You need to take it real slow."

A woman stood over her. A stout woman in a nurse's uniform, her smile bright against her dark skin, her eyes warm and sympathetic.

"Who....?" Courtney got out. "Where...?"

"Stay still," the nurse said, and carefully adjusted a pillow. "You're at the Thief River Falls Medical Center. I'm Nurse Ross."

"I'm in a hospital?" Courtney said in confusion. She looked about her. The room was clean and neat. An I.V. was beside the bed, monitors on the other side. Everything was so perfectly ordinary that for a few moments she hoped that maybe, just maybe, she had been having a nightmare about the end of the world and none of the terrible things she imagined had really happened. World War Three never broke out. Her mother and father and sister and brother were alive and well. So was Billy.

Nurse Ross shattered her delusion with, "Your friends brought you in. You've been unconscious for three days."

"Three days!" Courtney tried to sit up but the nurse restrained her.

"Cut that out. The doctor says you're lucky to be alive. You suffered a concussion and a dislocated shoulder and multiple contusions."

"Doctor?" Courtney repeated.

Nurse Ross nodded. "Doctor Parker. He and I are the only ones left. Most everyone else is either dead or fled."

Courtney glanced at the overhead light.

The nurse followed her gaze and said, "The doctor has the generator running. So long as we can find fuel, we can keep it going."

"My friends?" Courtney said.

"They're in rooms on the second floor," Nurse Ross said. "They're worried as can be. That boyfriend of yours spends all his time in here mooning over you. I shooed him out a while ago so he could get some sleep."

"He's not my....," Courtney began, and stopped.

"The little girl will be happy to hear you've come around," Nurse Ross continued. "She's cried up a storm, thinking you would die. Your friend Sally Ann has been pretty depressed, too."

"How did they find this place?"

"Dumb luck, from what they told me," Nurse Ross said. "They tore into town looking for medicine for you and saw a sign that pointed them here."

"Thanks goodness," Courtney said.

"Thank God, you mean," Nurse Ross said, and smiled. "Someone up above has been looking after you." She tucked the blanket and patted Courtney. "Now you just lay here, all right? You're nowhere near to being recovered. I'll go find the doctor so he can examine you, and I'll let your friends know you're back among the living."

That reminded Courtney. "What about the zombies and things? Can they get in here?"

"No. We keep the doors locked." Ross started out, pausing to say, "Rest, missy. You're in good hands, and safe."

Safe. Courtney very much doubted that was the case. She closed her eyes, and the next she knew, she was opening them again with the sense that a lot of time had passed.

A chair had been pulled next to the bed. Gar was in it, his hands clasped in his lap and his chin on his chest.

"Garland?" Courtney said, using his full first name and not sure why.

Gar shot to his feet and bent over her and smiled like she had never seen him smile before. "Sorry. Dozed off."

"Are you keeping watch over me?" she teased.

Gar nodded. "I'm in here every minute except when they chase me out."

Courtney slid her right arm out from under the blanket and he placed his hand on hers as if it were the most natural thing in the world to do. She stared at his hand and then at him. "What's going on with us?"

"I don't rightly know," Gar said. "Or maybe I do and

it spooks me a little."

"Well," Courtney said. She might have said more but there was a squeal of delight and Sansa ran up and practically threw herself onto the bed to hug her.

"Courtney! We were so worried!"

"Were we ever," Sally Ann said, coming up on the other side of the bed.

Gaga was wagging her tail fit to break it off.

"Together again," Courtney said happily.

Her good mood lasted for all of ten seconds.

That was when a loud crash resounded from somewhere not far off, and a shot boomed.

Gar was out the door in a flash, barking, "Stay with her!" to Sally Ann over his shoulder.

"You can go see what's going on if you want," Courtney said.

"No, he's right," Sally Ann said. "You're in no shape to defend yourself. I'll stay."

"What can it be?" Sansa worried.

Sally Ann put an arm around the girl's shoulders. "We'll know soon enough."

They waited in tense expectation, Courtney straining her ears for the slightest sounds. She heard voices in the distance but couldn't make out what they were saying and then nothing for the longest while.

All three of them gave a mild start when the door suddenly opened.

In walked a portly man in a white smock with glasses perched on the tip of his nose. He was carrying a clipboard. Smiling, he came over to the bed. "I finally get to say hello to my patient. I'm Doctor Parker. How are you feeling today?"

Courtney was more concerned about something else.

"That shot we heard?"

"Oh. That was me. I keep a shotgun in my office. One of the plague victims got in somehow, and I had to dispose of it."

"Plague victims?"

"That's what the doc calls the zombies," Sally Ann enlightened her.

"Your boyfriend is off checking the doors and windows to see how it got in," Dr. Parker said.

"He's not my....," Courtney began for the second time that day, and once again stopped.

The physician consulted the monitor and eyed the I.V. "You're quite the lucky young lady. If you're friends hadn't found us, you would have died. As it is, in ten days to two weeks you should be good as new, as they say."

"Two weeks!" Courtney gasped. "We have somewhere to be. I can't stay that long."

Parker chuckled. "Why is it patients can't wait to get out of the hospital that saved their life?" He motioned. "You want to leave? Be my guest. But be aware that without proper bed rest and nourishment you could suffer a relapse, and the next time you might not be so lucky."

"Don't sugarcoat it like that, Doc," Sally Ann joked. "Tell it to her straight."

Parker laughed.

"Back up," Courtney said. "What was that about a plague? I thought the zombies were caused by the chemical or biological weapons that were dropped on us?"

"Exactly so," Dr. Parker said. "Those weapons induced a plague of necro rejuvenation."

"Huh?"

"Making the dead come alive," Sally Ann said. "He's already explained it to me."

"Quite an effective stratagem, as we've seen for ourselves," Dr. Parker said. "An army of the dead to do our enemy's work for them."

Courtney scowled in disgust. To her, the entire idea of war, of killing other people, was flat out insane. Particularly killing people because of their politics or religion or race.

"Evil has long lurked in the hearts of humankind," Dr. Parker said. "It comes in many forms and guises."

The door opened again and Nurse Ross smiled at them. "Doctor, Gar found a busted window. He thinks that's how the creature got in, and he wants to know if we have a hammer and nails so he can board it over."

"Ah," Parker said. He touched Courtney's arm. "For your own sake, Ms. Hewitt, please reconsider leaving. I didn't go to all the trouble I did to preserve your life just to have you loose it because you're too stubborn for your own good." Out he whisked, the nurse tagging after him.

"You should listen," Sally Ann said. "The compound can wait."

"But ten days to two weeks!" Courtney said. She didn't know if she could lie still that long.

"While you're recuperating we'll hunt up another vehicle," Sally Ann said. "That mutation made a mess of the Mustang."

"Poor Gar. He liked it."

"Yes. Poor Gar," Sally Ann said dryly, and sighed. "Plus the nurse told us there are a couple of sporting goods stores that might not be picked over. We'll check them out when you're on your feet."

"I'd like some candy bars," Sansa said. "And doggie treats for Gaga."

"There you go," Sally Ann said. "Us girls will shop until we drop while you mend." She turned. "Come on, little one. She needs her rest."

"I'm glad you're okay," Sansa said. "'We're a family now and I would cry like crazy if we lost you."

Courtney was about to say that they were friends, not a family, but she didn't want to hurt Sansa's feeling.

For the longest time she lay there thinking about everything that had happened. About the compound. About Gar.

Especially about Gar.

Life was throwing stuff at her right and left.

Which begged the question: what next?

CHAPTER 27

It was ten days before Dr. Parker told Courtney she could get out of bed. It was another three before he said that she was fit enough to leave, but she must be careful not to overexert herself.

Courtney was practically giddy with glee. She couldn't wait to get out of there.

Gar was with her every day. So were Sally Ann and Sansa, although they did go shopping a few times.

Courtney mentioned time and again that they didn't need to watch over her but they were strangely reluctant to leave her alone.

Gar, Courtney could understand. He was making no secret of how he felt about her.

But Sally Ann and Sansa? Finally Courtney came right out and asked Sally why.

"Because we've learned the hard way not to take anything for granted. You seem safe. But there are no guarantees."

"I don't need a babysitter," Courtney joked. "Besides, the doc and the nurse are here."

"They're not family, like us," Sally Ann said.

That word again. Courtney would never have imagined her bestie being so sentimental, but then, times, to put it mildly, had changed.

As for Gar, Courtney learned a lot about him. For instance, his family had lived in Arkansas for generations. Poor folk, mostly, as he put it. Back in the

Old West days, an ancestor of his had gained notoriety as a gunfighter.

"I've sometimes wished I was born back then," Gar remarked.

"Why in the world would you?" Courtney said.

"Fewer laws. Fewer politicians. Life was simple then. More honest."

Courtney didn't see how. Her own life had been perfectly fine before the war broke out. Oh, there had been little things, like school, and her annoying brother, and her dad and mom getting on her case a lot. But overall, she'd had it pretty easy.

Then came the day of her release, and she was busting at the seams to go.

Dr. Parker and Nurse Ross were on hand to see her off.

Courtney gave each a hug even though she wasn't much for hugging people she barely knew.

Sally Ann and Sansa were happy, too. "At long last we can be on our way," her friend declared.

Parked out front was a new model van, the side door open, Gar leaning against the vehicle with his arms folded.

"Your chariot awaits, my lady."

"He had to do a lot of work to get it running," Sally Ann revealed. "It's roomy and comfy and has an in-dash TV."

"Not that we can get anything on it," Sansa said.

"Where are we off to?" Courtney wanted to know.

"The doc told us about a new shopping center," Gar said. "How do new clothes and whatever else your little heart desires sound?"

"What about the zombies?"

"We haven't seen any in days," Sally Ann said.

"First, though, sporting goods," Gar said.

The van had a 'new car' smell. Courtney melted into the middle seat and breathed deep, glad to be shed of the hospital odors.

The sporting goods store wasn't far.

Courtney was perlexed to see several tall metal constructs out front. She'd never seen anything like them.

"Tree stands," Gar informed her. "For hunters."

Amazingly, the store appeared to be untouched. The windows were intact, the front door locked. Gar knocked and rattled the window but no one came.

"Can't believe this place hasn't been looted," Sally Ann remarked.

"I'll bust the door in," Gar said.

"What if there's a back way?" Courtney said.

There was. And it was unlocked.

Drawing his revolver, Gar opened it enough to poke his head in. "Black as pitch." He let out a yell. "Anyone to home?"

"It's a store, silly," Sansa said. She was holding onto Gaga's collar.

Sunlight streamed in through a barred window high on the wall. They were in a storage room lined with shelves piled with merchandise.

"We've hit the jackpot," Gar said.

Courtney crossed to a door to the store proper. She turned the knob, eager to get her hands on a new shotgun.

The thing that reared in the doorway had hands, too, which it curled toward her throat.

It was a female zombie, emaciated to mere skin and

bones. Its glazed eyes reflected the sunlight streaming into the storage room. Its teeth---uneven and rotting---gaped as it lunged.

Courtney screamed. She couldn't help herself. Instinctively, she backpedaled and swatted at the creature's hands to keep them from touching her.

The zombie came at her again.

Courtney tried to leap out of reach, and tripped. To keep from falling, she flung an arm against a shelf.

The boom of a revolver was thunder in her ears.

Gar had rushed up and at point-blank range, shot the hideous caricature of humanity in the forehead.

"That was close!" Sally Ann said. She nudged the horror at their feet. "Whoever this was must have been stuck in here since everything went to hell."

"Poor lady," Sansa said.

"There might be more," Gar said. "Let me go first." He entered the store with his revolver extended in a two-handed grip, which for him was unusual.

Sally Ann took hold of Courtney's upper arm. "Can you walk? Do you need help?"

Courtney shook her head, and followed them in. One look, and she agreed with Gar. They had indeed hit the jackpot. Everything was exactly as it had been when the bombs and s rained down.

A wealth of sporting goods was theirs for the taking. From tents to fishing poles, from lanterns to backpacks. Firearms, ammo, they could take their pick.

Gar went straight to the gun racks. "Look here! There are several semi-autos."

"Several what?" Sansa said.

"Assault rifles," Gar said. "They let you shoot a lot of rounds fast. We can use the firepower if we run into another swarm."

"Too bad there aren't any machine guns," Sally Ann said. She sounded serious.

Courtney examined the handguns in a row of display cases. She spied a revolver like Gar's, only larger, and beckoned him over. "I'd like this one. It's big enough to stop any zombie that comes along."

Gar chuckled. "Got that right. Although it's the caliber, not the size of the gun, that matters more. This is a .44 Magnum."

"Meaning?"

"It kicks like a bucking horse," Gar said. "Unless you have a lot of practice, it can be hard to aim. You might miss more than you hit."

"How about this one, then?" Courtney pointed at a pistol with white grips.

"A .357 Magnum," Gar said. "It won't kick as much as the .44, but still."

"What would you suggest, then?"

"A caliber that will drop a zombie if you hit it in the right spot, but one that is easier for a shooter your size to control." Gar tapped the glass above a matched pair of autopistols. "These should do you fine. They're 9 millimeter parabellums. Good stopping power but you don't need arms of steel to hold them steady."

Courtney trusted his judgement. He also picked something called an AR-15 for her 'shoulder weapon'. It had a twenty-round magazine and came with a collapsible stock.

Everyone, even Sansa, ended up armed to the gills.

Operating under the theory that 'We can never have enough firepower!', Gar proceeded to fill duffel bags with enough guns and ammo to outfit an army.

By Courtney's count, they lugged seven heavy bags out to the van.

Surveying their plunder, Gar smiled and remarked, "This should get us to the compound, easy."

"Provided, of course, that the compound is still there," Sally Ann said.

"Why wouldn't it be?" Courtney said.

"The end of the world, remember?" Sally Ann said. "There's no guarantee those survivalists are still alive. They might have been overrun by a swarm or done in by a chemical cloud."

"Focus on the bright side, why don't you?" Courtney said.

"Ladies, ladies," Gar said. "There's only one way to find out. Hop in and let's hit that shopping center for the clothes you want. Then we're off to Lake Bronson State Park. Shouldn't take us more than a day to get there."

"From your mouth to God's ears," Sally Ann said.

CHAPTER 28

Courtney hoped the final leg of their journey would go easier. She was encouraged that the first few miles out of Thief River Falls, they didn't spot a single zombie.

Sansa was in good spirits, and humming to herself.

Sally Ann was lost in thought.

Courtney faced toward Gar. "I want to thank you for all you've been doing for us."

"I'd do it for anybody."

"Really?"

"No," Gar said, and laughed. "I like you. I like your friends. I could see right away that you're good people."

"And that's important?"

"Do you even need to ask after all you've told me you've been through? The world is so screwed up, it might never recover. There were a lot of bad folks before the war. Now the bad is everywhere."

"By bad you mean....?" Courtney prompted.

"Evil," Gar said. "Some people scoff. They say there's no such thing. No right. No wrong. No good. No evil. That's bull. Putting people in gas chambers is evil. Blowing them up because they don't practice the same religion is evil. Molesting kids is evil. I could go on and on."

"Yes, there's evil," Courtney agreed, thinking of some of the vicious sorts she had run into since leaving Minneapolis.

"A lot of folks don't want to admit it exists. They'd rather pretend it doesn't. They close their eyes to it and imagine the world is a pretty place filled with friendly sorts who would never harm a fly. Why fight evil when you can ignore it?"

"My, my" Courtney said. "That's about the most I've heard you say at one time since we met. I take it that you feel strongly about it?"

"If people had cared more, we wouldn't be in this mess. If they had stood up for what was right and not let the politicians con them into turning the other cheek until there was nowhere left to turn...." Gar stopped. "Sorry. I can get carried away. It riles me, is all, how those in power betrayed their trust."

"It's nice to be passionate about something."

Gar glanced over. "It's not the only thing I'm passionate about."

Courtney was sure she blushed. To cover her embarrassment she gazed out the window. She needed to make up her mind what she was going to do. Namely, hook up with him, or not. He'd made his feelings plain. She should do the same.

But what *were* her feelings? She liked him. Liked him a lot. He was hot. He was courteous. He treated her with respect. But did she want him in the way he plainly wanted her?

Sighing, Courtney leaned her forehead against the cool glass. Decisions, decisions and more decisions. Ever since the war, she was forced to make up her mind about one thing after another, important things. Matters of life and death. And now this.

She put it from her mind for the time being and tried to relax and enjoy the ride. Even with the roiling clouds, the day was peaceful, almost picturesque. She lost track of time and was startled when Sally Ann extended her arm over the seat and pointed.

"See that sign? Lake Bronson State Park is up ahead!"

"Where exactly is the compound?" Gar asked. "In the Park?"

"On the outskirts, according to the radio we heard," Sally Ann said.

"Do we stay on 10 or take 28?" Gar wanted to know.

Sally Ann glanced at Courtney. "What's your guess?"

"No idea," Courtney admitted. The broadcast hadn't been specific.

"Great," Gar said.

"My suggestion is to circle the park, sticking to the closest roads," Sally Ann proposed. "If the compound is nearby, we should come across it."

"Unless they don't want to be found," Gar said.

"Huh?" Sansa said.

"Think about it, little one," Gar said. "From what I've been told, this place was set up by a survivalist. Someone who saw the end coming and took steps to try and stay alive. Someone who might want to keep it a secret. I'm surprised it was on the radio."

"The news report said a hunter came across it," Sally Ann clarified.

"Which means it has to be well off the beaten path," Gar said.

"What's that?" Sansa said.

"He means it might be well hid," Courtney said.

"Gosh, I hope we find it," the girl said. "I want to be somewhere where I don't have to worry all the time."

"Don't we all," Sally Ann said softly.

Courtney became tense with expectation. She yearned to find a haven, somewhere the zombies and the mutants and the monsters couldn't get at them. God, that would be sweet!

For the next couple of hours they prowled up one back road and down another. It wasn't easy to stay close to the Park.

Evening was approaching when Gar suddenly slammed on the brakes, causing all of them to lurch forward.

"What was that for?" Sally Ann said.

Gar nodded at a tract of woods. The tree line was unbroken save for a swath as wide as a vehicle where the vegetation had been crushed flat. Tire tracks showed here and there.

"Someone has made their own road," Sally Ann said.

"Where does it go?" Sansa wondered.

"The million dollar question," Gar said, and wheeled into it. "Let's find out."

The track wound through the woods with no seeming rhyme or reason that Courtney could see until of a sudden they climbed to the crest of a low hill, and there, about a quarter of a mile away, past more forest, sprawled a compound with high walls and---of all things---a drawbridge. The drawbridge was up, and a wide cleared space in front of it was filled with tents.

Inside the walls were enormous concrete structures, only their roofs visible.

"There!" Sally Ann exclaimed, pointing. "That has to be it!"

"It's so big," Sansa said. "Look how long those walls are."

"Twenty to thirty acres would be my guess," Gar

said. His window was down and had stuck his head out for a better view.

"They should have plenty of room for us, then," Courtney said. She shouldn't get her hopes up but the prospect of a safe haven had her tingling with excitement.

Gar followed the track down the hill. Trees closed in on either side, hemming their van. They had only gone a short way when he slammed on the brakes.

A fallen tree blocked them. A small tree with a lot of leaves.

Gar leaned out, saying, "That shouldn't be a problem. I can move it myself." He went to climb out.

From seemingly out of nowhere men appeared. Men dressed in orange jumpsuits. Over a dozen, armed with rifles and shotguns and handguns.

Gar's hand flicked to his Colt but a hulking man with huge shoulders pressed the muzzle of a rifle to Gar's temple.

"So much as twitch and I'll splatter your brains."

Courtney could tell that Gar was tempted to try something. "Don't!" she said, "Please!"

Gar's eyes shifted to the ring of firearms trained on her and Sally Ann and Sansa.

"Listen to the lady," the hulking man said. "Otherwise every one of you dies."

Gar frowned, and splayed his fingers to show he wouldn't resist.

"Smart," the man said.

Sally Ann was furious. "What do you want? What's the meaning of this?"

"You're kidding, right?" the man said.

Courtney's door was pulled open and a man with a

face that made her think of a weasel reached in, grabbed her arm, and roughly hauled her out. She went to hit him but he waggled a pistol in her face and said, "Better not, bitch."

Gaga growled and the man pointed his pistol but Courtney quickly shielded Gaga with her body. "Don't! Please! Gaga, stay still!"

Sally Ann, Sansa and Gar were lined up against the driver's side. Gar was disarmed.

Shoved by the weasel, Courtney was forced to join them.

All of the men in orange stood regarding them coldly. Their apparent leader, the hulking man,went from Sally Ann to Sansa to Gar to Courtney, looking each of them up and down. Finally he grunted.

"These should do us," he said.

"What are you talking about?" Sally Ann said. "Who are you, anyhow?"

"You sure got a mouth on you," the man said. "But I'll explain, just so you know what we want and what will happen if you don't do what we say." He paused. "I'm Luther. These are my friends." He gestured at the others. Several grinned as if it were a joke. "We were part of a work crew when the world went to hell. Our guards were taking us back to prison but they were worried about their families and got careless and, well....."

The man Courtney thought of as Weasel gave a bark of a laugh. "No more guards!"

Luther pointed in the direction of the compound. "We heard about the place you were heading for. Figured we would see if we could sneak in and make it ours."

"What?" Courtney said. "Why?"

"They're not about to let us waltz on in, us being convicts, and all. So we're going to take it over. Kill their guards and their leaders, and the rest will fall in line."

"Just the fourteen of you?" Sally Ann said.

"There are only about a hundred in there, best we could count by sneaking close," Luther said. "Many are women and kids. We get rid of most of the men, and bingo."

"It's all ours," Weasel said.

"So here we were," Luther resumed, "trying to figure out how to get one of us inside to scope out the place, when yours van came along."

"We'll never help you!" Sally Ann said.

"Oh, really?" Luther said. He pointed his rifle at Sansa.

CHAPTER 29

The convict doing the driving was named Spit. Why anyone would let themselves be called that, Courtney had no idea.

Spit's was the same size as Gar, and he was now wearing one of Gar's extra shirts and jeans. He was also driving the van, and kept glancing suspiciously over at her.

"You better not mess this up, girl."

"I won't," Courtney assured him.

"Better not," Spit stressed. "You do, and I don't make it back, you can kiss your friends goodbye. Even the little one. Luther won't think twice about blowing her away."

"I know what I'm supposed to do," Courtney said angrily.

Spit gazed ahead at the compound and the field surrounding it.. "We'll go over this again anyway. I'm your dad. We're with a bunch of other people from the Twin Cities. We heard about this place and we came ahead to check it out."

"You're crazy to try and take the place over," Courtney said. "You know that, don't you?"

"What I know is that you'd best behave," Spit said irritably. "They let us in, I can find out what we're up against, and report back to Luther."

"Isn't the world in enough of a mess?" Courtney said. "Why can't everyone get along?"

"Dream on, girl. I'm no big brain, but I know that people have been at each other's throats since there were, well, people. It's dog eat dog."

"It didn't use to be," Courtney said.

"Before the war, you mean? Hell. You bought the whole fairy tale, didn't you? Yeah, sure, before the war people were forced to get along whether they wanted to or not. All those laws. All those police." Spit snickered. "You think all of that would have been needed if people *could* get along?"

"It was called being civilized," Courtney said.

"What good did that do us? Hello? World War Three?" Spit shook his head. "No, civilized just meant people were kept in cages but didn't realize it because they couldn't see the bars."

They were nearing the cleared area. Thirty tents or more, of all different sizes and colors and kinds, dotted the field. Most were close to the drawbridge as if for protection.

People were lounging or cooking. Some kids were playing.

"Doesn't look as if many are getting in," Spit remarked.

Courtney could see figures on the ramparts.

A big blond man was watching them approach through binoculars.

Spit nodded at a stream that entered the walls via an aqueduct. "That must be how they get their water. We might be able to slip in that way." He thoughtfully gnawed on his bottom lip. "It explains the drawbridge. It opens inward, over the stream."

A lot of the people around the tents were staring at the van.

"Remember, smile and act real nice and friendly," Spit said. "One slip and...."

"You don't have to keep reminding me," Courtney snapped.

When they were about forty feet out from the compound, Spit braked and put the van in Park. Showing all of his teeth, he opened his door and climbed out with his arms in the air.

Courtney followed suit.

"Hello up there!" Spit hollered. "We're peaceful!"

The blond man had lowered his binoculars. His hair was shoulder-length, and tied back. He sported a thick mustache and a trimmed beard."What do you want?"

"We heard about this place on the radio," Spit shouted up. "Me and the rest from Minneapolis."

The blond man stared toward the woods. "The rest?"

"They're a ways back yet," Spit said. "They sent me ahead."

"How many?" the blond man said.

"Twenty-five," Spit lied, and added, "Ten are kids."

The blond man frowned. "That radio report again." He didn't sound happy about it.

"I'm Richard, by the way," Spit said. "Who might you be?"

"Soren."

"Do you run this place?"

"No. I'm a Warrior."

"A what?"

"A Warrior," Soren repeated. "We defend the Home."

"The what?"

"It's what the Family calls the compound."

"The who?"

The Warrior cocked his head and gave Spit a strange look.

Spit said, "So will you let us in, or what?"

"That's not for me to decide," Soren said. "I'll go find the man who runs things. It'll be his call."

Courtney realized the blond man was studying her intently. She forced a smile. "Thank you!"

The Warrior turned and was gone.

"So far, so good," Spit said.

To Courtney's considerable surprise, she knew the man who was introduced as the leader of the survivalists. Not personally. She had never met him. But she had seen him occasionally on the news. He was a Hollywood bigshot.

A loud clanking noise had risen from beyond the wall, and the drawbridge was slowly lowered. As it was descending, Courtney could see that a wedge of well-armed men, including Soren, had formed around another man---and a woman---and at that man's gesture, they crossed the drawbridge, their guns at the ready.

All except Soren. He was carrying a huge hammer covered in strange symbols. Up close, Courtney saw that he was wearing some sort of rubber suit that reminded her of the suits scuba divers wore. He also had on odd gloves and a bizarre belt about his middle that had dials and stuff on it.

The group came to the end of the drawbridge, and the famous man halted. "This will do, Thor."

Courtney noticed that people were coming from the tents to watch. She ignored them for now and focused on the bigshot.

"Thor?" Spit said. "I thought the dude told us his name is Soren?"

"Thor is his code name," the famous man said. He was quite handsome, and his voice gentle, almost weary. "All the Warriors have them."

"Are there a lot of these Warriors?" Spit asked.

Paying him no heed, the famous man came toward Courtney and extended his hand. "Kurt Carpenter. A pleasure to meet you, young lady."

Courtney introduced herself as they shook.

Carpenter indicated the woman beside him. "This is my associate, Diana Trevor."

Again Courtney shook. Trevor had friendly but wary eyes, and dark hair. On the slim side, she was dressed in a shirt and slacks.

"We understand that you two are part of a group from the Twin Cities?" the woman said.

"That's right, sister," Spit said. "With ten kids," he stressed.

"How far off are they?" Diana Trevor wanted to know.

Spit shrugged. "About a day out, I suppose."

Kurt Carpenter sighed. He gazed at the the people among the tents and said, "They just keep coming."

"It's that radio station," Soren---or was it Thor?---said. "The one that found out about us and kept broadcasting for days after the war."

His tone prompted Courtney to say, "You make that sound like a bad thing."

Kurt Carpenter's features grew sad. "It's a contingency I didn't anticipate."

"Sorry?" Courtney said.

"When I realized war was inevitable, when I planned

for the Home, as we call it," Carpenter explained, "I worked everything out to the smallest detail. Including how many people the Home could hold. It was invitation only, based on certain criteria."

"With no room for any more?" Spit said. "As much ground as you have in there?"

"It's not the space considerations," Carpenter said. "We have provisions for a set number of people to last a set number of years. Should we add more mouths to feed....," Carpenter didn't finish.

"You'll run out of supplies sooner," Courtney said.

"Surely you can take a few more in?" Spit said.

Carpenter indicated the tent people. "There are already dozens waiting their chance. Now your groups shows up. And not one of you has been vetted."

"Huh?" Spit said.

Diana Trevor said, "None of you have had a background investigation, your DNA profiled...."

"That science stuff?" Spit said.

Trevor went on as if he hadn't interrupted. "Your education levels, criminal records, those sorts of things."

Kurt Carpenter said, "The people in the Home were chosen using a computer program."

"So you'd let the rest of us sit out here and starve?" Spit said. "Or be killed by zombies or some other thing?"

"I haven't made up my mind yet," Carpenter said. "Until I do, you and the rest of your group are welcome to camp outside our walls. We'll provide you with food, medicine and protection."

"How about a tour?" Spit said.

"I'm afraid that's out of the question," Carpenter

said.

"Well, hell," Spit said.

Carpenter half-turned to go. "I hope to reach a decision soon."

Diana Trevor smiled at Courtney. "Nice to have met you."

Courtney couldn't say what motivated her to do what she did next. Taking a quick step, she hugged Trevor close, saying loudly, "Nice meeting you, too!" Instantly she whispered into the woman 's ear, "Help us, please! Four of us are being held by that man and other convicts! They want to take over your compound!" She stepped back, keeping a happy expression, worried sick that Spit had heard her.

But no.

He was already heading for the van.

Diana Trevor hadn't let on what Courtney had done. Her smile widened and she said, "Don't you worry, Ms Hewitt. Things will work out."

"I sure hope so," Courtney said.

CHAPTER 30

All her life Courtney had heard the expression 'a nervous wreck'. But she never actually experienced being one---until now.

As the van wound through the woods towards where they had left the others, Courtney tried not to fidget or wring her hands or otherwise give herself away.

Spit was mad, but not at her. "That miserable son of a bitch! Who does he think he is, anyway? He wouldn't even let us take a peek inside those walls."

Courtney laughed.

"What the hell's so funny?" Spit said.

Nothing, really, except that Courtney's nerves were on edge. "Maybe he thought you have cooties."

"This is serious, stupid," Spit said. "Luther ain't going to like that I couldn't scout the place out. Knowing him, it'll make him more determined ever to get in and take it over. Which means he might forget scouting it out. Which means," he said with a sneer, "that we might not have any more use for you and your friends."

"He'd kill us in cold blood?"

"Just like that," Spit said, and snapped his fingers.

"God," Courtney said, bowing her head. "There's just no end to this nightmare."

"Grow up, girl. It is what it is."

"That's no excuse for what you and your friends are doing."

"We're looking out for number one. Ourselves."

"That's cold."

"That's smart. You need to face up to the fact that no one is around to take care of you anymore. Not mommy. Not daddy. Not the government."

"I know that," Courtney said bitterly.

"It's like that nursery rhyme. What's it called? Humpty Dumpty? About the egg that falls and goes splat. Well, now the whole world has, and nothing you do can ever put it back together again. Now it's survival of the strongest."

"You think you're strong?"

"Strength in numbers, bitch," Spit said. "Me and my buds, we're at the top of the food chain."

"The people at the compound are."

"They didn't strike me as all that much," Spit said. "We find a way in, they're toast."

Courtney hoped not. Carpenter and his followers had impressed her as decent people. She prayed they would take her request for help seriously.

Presently they reached the camp the convicts had set up. Spit's orange-clad companions converged.

"Your back sooner than I figured," Luther said. Strapped around his waist were Gar's holster and Colt.

"They wouldn't let us in," Spit reported, and launched into an explanation as to why.

Luther wasn't pleased. "So you have no idea how many of these Warriors we'd be up against?"

"Nope," Spit admitted. "I saw six guys with weapons with the head honcho but only the big one looked all that tough. And he was carrying a hammer."

"Say that again?" Luther said.

"I kid you not," Spit said. "No gun. Just some weird-ass hammer, and wearing an outfit that looked to be made of rubber." Spit snorted in contempt. "You ask me, they're a bunch of candy asses."

"I don't get the hammer bit," Luther said. "But hey. If they're too stupid to pack guns, it'll be easier for us." He motioned at the others. "We're going to sit down and hash out how to make that compound our own."

Spit jabbed Courtney in the arm. "What about the babe here? And her friend? Any reason we can't have some fun with them later?"

Luther grinned. "None at all."

The rope hurt terribly. Her skin on both wrists was scraped raw and she was bleeding. But she refused to stop trying to work free.

The convicts had bound her and the others. One of them held a gun to her face while Spit did the deed. He kept licking his lips and winking. When he was done, he patted her head and said, "Later, babe. You and me."

"And me," leered the guy holding the gun.

Now, curled on her side facing the fire, her arms behind her, Courtney grit her teeth and twisted her wrists for all she was worth.

Sally Ann and Sansa lay nearby. Gar, though, had been tied to a tree.

Even Gaga was on a stake.

Sally Ann was doing twisting of her own. She looked over and whispered despondently, "It never ends, does it?"

Grunting, Courtney kept at the rope.

"We were almost to the compound, and now this," Sally Ann said.

"Don't give up hope,"

Sally Ann glared at the convicts, who were passing bottles of whiskey around and talking and joking. "God. I can't stand the thought of them touching me."

"They haven't yet," Courtney said. "And so long as I'm breathing, I'll be damned if they will."

"When did you become so tough?" Sally Ann said. "When the war broke out, it was me who had to keep boosting your spirits."

"I don't know," Courtney said, continuing to work at her bounds. "I just grew tougher, I guess."

"Shape up or die? Should that be our new motto?"

Courtney wished her friend would stop distracting her. She was to say as much when she saw Luther stand up and come around the fire. She pressed her wrists against her butt to hide her wrists, and tensed.

"How are you ladies holding up?" Luther said amiably. He took a swig from a bottle, then held it out toward Sally Ann. "Care for a swallow?"

"Go to hell," Sally Ann said.

"That's not too smart," Luther said. "Make me mad, why don't you? Make the others mad, too. So when the time comes, we'll smack you around while we're getting our jollies."

"You're despicable."

"People have needs, girl."

"Loathsome."

Luther took another swig. "You really need to get your act together. Unless you *want* to die. In which case, go on being a bitch."

Courtney had something else on her mind. "What about Sansa?"

"The kid?" Luther said. "What does she...." He

stopped. "Oh, hell. None of us are child molesters, if that's what you're getting at."

"She shouldn't have see it," Courtney said. "Shouldn't even have to hear it."

Luther swallowed more whiskey, and nodded. "Yeah. Good point. I'll have her put in the van."

"Thanks," Courtney said.

"Now see?" Luther said to Sally Ann. "Why can't you be nice like her?" He started to turn, and stopped. "Either of you hungry? Want some of the meat?"

"What are you having?" Sally Ann said.

"Dog."

Courtney stiffened. "Wait. What?" She glanced anxiously at Gaga. "You can't mean.....?"

"Won't be our first," Luther said. "Has a nice taste once you get used to it."

"You can't eat Gaga!" Struggling to sit up, Courtney said, "Please, no! She's been with me since before we left Minneapolis."

"As if we care," Luther said..

Courtney looked at Gaga and tears welled. She really and truly cared for her. "I'll do anything! Please! I'm begging you!"

A muscular black man with the sleeves cut off his jumpsuit came over. "What's all the fuss, Luth?"

"Hey, Malik," Luther said, and held out the bottle to him. "This one doesn't want us to eat her dog."

"Maybe she rather we eat her," Malik said, and they both chuckled.

Courtney's dismay gave way to anger. "Harm her, and so help me, I'll tear your throats out with my teeth!"

"You're welcome to try," Malik said.

"Ah, hell, girl," Luther said. "Don't take it so personal."

"Bitches and their mutts," Malik said. "I had me a ho once who went everywhere with a tiny little poodle in her purse."

"Bastards!"

"You know what?" Malik said. "How about I do the dog right now?" And with that, he drew a broad-bladed knife from a sheath on his hip.

CHAPTER 31

Courtney tried to stand but lost her balance and fell back. "Leave my dog alone!"

Malik made small circles in the air with the tip of his blade. "How about I bring you a piece to eat raw?"

Luther laughed.

It was then that Gar Shannon said, "Miserable pukes,."

The two convicts faced the tree.

"You got something to say, mister?" Luther said.

Gar said, "My pa used to say that convicts and pond scum have a lot in common. Now I know what he meant."

"Say what?" Malik said.

"Are you hard of hearing as well as dumb?" Gar said.

"You believe this fool?" Malik asid to Luther.

Gar went on. "Between the two of you, you don't have enough brains to fit in a pea."

Luther snorted. "Is that your idea of an insult?"

"Take a gander in a mirror," Gar said. "Your face is an insult."

"Gander?" Malik said. He glanced at Luther. "What's this cracker think he's doing?"

"He's trying to get under our skin," Luther said. "Maybe hoping it will delay us doing the dog."

Courtney wanted to reach out and hug Gar.

"That's not why I'm doing it at all," Gar said. "I just hate cowards. And the two of you got no more gonads than a clam."

"That made no sense," Malik said.

"Let me be plain," Gar said, glaring at Luther. "Cut me free and let you and me have a fair fight so I can beaet you into the ground and make you whimper like those dogs you like to eat."

"You and me?" Luther said. "Hand to hand?"

"Fool," Malik said to Gar. "Luth, here, was the best fighter in the whole prison."

"Let him prove it," Gar said, raising his voice. "Or is he scared to?"

Some of the other convicts stopped what they were doing to listen.

"You heard me, Luther!" Gar practically shouted. "I'm calling you a yellow-dog coward! You're afraid to take me on! You're afraid I'll kick your ass!"

Now all the convicts were listening. Several stood and came over and the rest followed.

"That's right!" Gar taunted. "Have your pards back you up because you're too much of a wimp to take me on yourself."

Malik waggled his knife. "Let me do him for you, Luth."

"You hear that?" Gar yelled at the others. "Your big, bad leader has to have somebody else do his fighting."

"Mister," Spit said, "we've seen him kill men a lot bigger and tougher than you."

"You don't look like much at all," another convict said.

"Cut me loose and I'll show you," Gar said.

Courtney felt a wave of worry wash over her. "Gar, don't make them mad. I don't want to lose you."

"Ah, ain't that sweet?" Malik said.

Luther placed his hand on the Colt at his waist.

"I don't care how mad they get," Gar said. "Where I come from, men don't take being insulted. They stand up for themselves." He regarded Luther with contempt. "Best fighter in the whole prison, huh? Who'd you fight? The nurses and secretaries?"

Luther took a step toward him.

In fear for Gar's life, Courtney gave a powerful wrench on her wrists and suddenly her right arm, slick with her blood, slipped free. Without thinking she threw herself at Luther and punched him on the jaw. He barely seemed to feel it, but was riveted in surprise. She swung again, then lunged at the holster to try and wrest the pistol free.

Luther exploded. His fist slammed into her belly, doubling her over. Staggering, she was unable to protect herself as his other fist swung up and around. There was a sharp blow to her head, and the next she knew, she was on her knees, bile in her mouth. The world spun crazily.

"Courtney!" Sansa screamed.

Her vision clearing, Courtney looked up. Convicts were grinning and laughing in amusement.

"Grab her," Luther said.

Spit and another man leaped to obey, each seizing one of Courtney's arms and yanking her to her feet.

Luther stepped up and jabbed her in the gut, hard. "You just made up my mind for me. We can use some entertainment, right boys?"

There were nods and yips of assent.

Luther cupped Courtney's chin, and squeezed. "So I'm not only going to fight your boyfriend. I'm going to fight you, too. The both of you at the same time."

He gave her head a violent shake. "I'm going to bust your bones."

With a lot of whooping and hollering, the convicts formed a circle to watch the fun.

The pair holding Courtney let go and she fell to her knees.

Luther unbuckled Gar's gunbelt and handed it to Spit. Then he went into a boxing stance and threw several short, powerful punches and jabs.

"Looking good, bro!" Malik said.

"Cut me loose," Gar said.

"When I'm good and ready," Luther said. He stepped up to Courtney and jabbed in the chest. "I bet you feel pretty stupid right about now."

"Go to hell," Courtney said.

"You shouldn't have attacked me. Say you're sorry and I'll let you off the hook."

"Go to hell twice," Courtney said.

Luther scowled. "You're one stupid bitch, you know that? I'm giving you a chance to bow out."

Malik pointed his knife at her. "Why are you being so nice to this cow?"

"I beat on her, she won't be in much shape to be poked later."

"Oh. Thought maybe you were going soft," Malik said.

"Not in this life," Luther said. Without warning, he suddenly grabbed Courtney by the hair, twisted, and flung her to the ground.

Pain spiked Courtney's neck and side but she refused to give them the satisfaction of showing it. Gritting her teeth, she sat up. "We've started already? You didn't say one, two, three, go."

"I'm just loosening up for the main event," Luther said.

Gar was straining against his ropes in fury. "Try that on me, you miserable wretch."

Luther smirked. "Malik, cut the bastard loose."

"Sure thing."

Squatting in front of Gar, Malik flashed his knife close to Gar's face, then pretended to stab him in the eye. Gar didn't flinch. Chuckling, Malik reached around, and with a single stroke, severed the rope. Slowly rising, he held his knife as if daring Gar to try something.

"Come on," Malik mocked him. "You know you want to."

Gar was glaring at Luther. "It's him I want. Not his sock puppet."

"What the hell did you call me?" Malik said.

"He's trying to set us against each other," Luther said. "Ignore him. He won't be breathing much longer."

"Why don't you let me do him and you do the girl?" Malik said.

"It was me he insulted," Luther said. "It was me she hit."

Reluctantly, Malik backed away. "Don't kill him Luth. Leave some for me."

Another convict exclaimed, "Can we get to it, already? The rate things are going, it'll be midnight before anyone throws a punch."

"What your hurry, Dyson?" Luther said. He didn't wait for an answer but planted himself about a yard from Gar and placed his hands on his hips. "On your feet, punk."

Gar rose, shaking his arms and legs as he did. "Cut off my circulation."

"Cry us a river," Luther said.

Courtney was waiting her chance. Not at Luther, at a gun. If she could get her hands on one, she could turn the tables, maybe keep the convicts covered while Gar freed Sally Ann and Sansa.

The one called Dyson was closest. He had a shotgun, cradled protectively in both arms.

Courtney decided the youngest of the convicts, to her right, was her best bet. He was absorbed in what Luther was doing, and holding a rifle loose in one hand.

Luther glowered at Gar and then at her. "Let's dance."

CHAPTER 32

Courtney kept forgetting how quick Gar was. When he drew, his hand was always a blur. And sometimes when he moved, like now, he was almost too fast for the eye to follow.

Gar swept in at Luther with his fists cocked as if he were going to box but at the last split-instant he tucked at the knees and hit Luther in the knee.

Luther cried out and his leg nearly buckled. He swiveled, flicked a right that Gar sidestepped, and drove a straight left at Gar's head. Gar ducked, pivoted, and struck Luther twice.

Luther was bigger and Luther had much more muscle but he was molasses compared to the Gar.

Again Luther swung, his blow passing over Gar's shoulder. Gar retaliated with a sharp jab to Luther's cheek that jarred him, and followed through with a looping right.

Luther skipped back out of reach.

To a man, the convicts were glued to the fight. Their faces glowed with a lust for violence.

Gar circled, and Luther mirrored him.

Luther spat and said, "You've been lucky so far."

Gar didn't respond.

"It won't last," Luther said.

"Do you ever shut up?" Gar said.

Luther reddened, and waded in with his fists flying. He was seeking to overpower Gar, to batter him into submission, but once again Gar was too quick. Gar took a punch to the arm and another to the ribs but he evaded most of the blow, twisting and dodging and ducking.

The convicts were cheering for Luther, some pumping their arms and waving their weapons.

Courtney's moment had come. No one was paying attention to her. She sidled toward the young one with the rifle----only to have him level the barrel at her and shake his head in warning.

Courtney froze.

Luther was trying to slip in close to Gar but Gar was proving to be as elusive as a ghost.

Luther's frustration mounted; his swings became wider and wilder.

Gar tripped. To Courtney, it looked as if he fell over his own feet. He ended up on his knees with one hand flat on the ground.

Luther sprang in and raised his right fist like a club.

Gar thrust his free arm up as if to ward off the blow. But it was a ruse.

As Luther's fist swept down, Gar threw himself at Spit. Caught flat-footed, all Spit could do was bleat in amazement as Gar slammed his left fist into Spit's middle. Spit doubled over.

In that instant, Gar's right hand flashed to his pearl-handled Colt in the holster that Spit held.

Gar spun, and as he started his turn, he fanned his Colt. His first shot caught Luther high in the forehead and snapped his head back. His second drilled Malik in the chest. His third felled Dyson. Gar continued to turn---but Malik hadn't gone down, and was rushing at him with the knife. Gar shot him in the throat. Still

Malik stayed on his feet. Gar fanned his pistol yet again and Malik's eye vanished in a geyser of gore.

Five shots, in less than half as many seconds.

The rest of the convicts galvanized to life and closed on Gar.

"No!" Courtney screamed. She threw herself at a pair of convicts and rained punches at their backs and heads to keep them from getting to Gar. One of them backhanded her and tottered.

Someone wrapped his hands around her neck.

It was Spit. His mouth twisted in glee, he bore her to the ground.

Courtney lost sight of Gar. He was down, being bludgeoned by four or five convicts at once. They weren't going to shoot him. They were going to beat him to death.

Sansa shrieked in terror.

Sally Ann yelled something.

And then the world was lit by lightning.

The flash was so bright, it hurt Courtney's eyes. For a moment she thought it had come from the sky.

But no.

A towering man had joined the melee, a man with golden hair and a golden beard, dressed in skintight black. It was Soren Anderson, the Warrior from the compound. In his right hand he wielded a hammer unlike any hammer ever made, and from it shot bolts and arcs of sizzling electricity. He pointed it at a convict holding a revolver and lightning leaped from the hammer to the revolver and up the convict's arm. The convict screamed, his eyes bulging, as his body whipped in a bow and smoke rose from his flesh.

Another convict rushed to his friend's aid, jerking a

rifle to his shoulder intending to shoot the golden-haired giant in the back.

From out of the darkness appeared a tall man in a trench coat. He had black hair and the bluest of blues eyes, and a submachine gun. He fired a short burst, riddling the convict from throat to groin.

At the same moment a third Warrior materialized. Dressed in fatigues and combat boots, he let loose with autofire.

A trio of convicts had turned on Soren Anderson. Instead of striking them, he thrust his hammer at the heavens and bellowed "Odin!" His thumb pressed a large stud on the handle, and crackling arcs of death leaped from the hammer's head to the heads of the three convicts. They died in midstep, blistered and shrieking.

The man in the trench coat fired.

So did the man in fatigues.

And just like that, it was over.

Courtney took in the sight of convincts sprawled in death. She saw movement under two of the bodies. "Gar!"

Spattered with blood and marked with bruises, his face was a testament to his struggle. He pushed one of the bodies off, mustered a smile, and said wearily, "Courts."

Courtney rolled the second body away, and dropped to a knee. "Let me help you."

Gar gestured, as if to wave her away. "No, I'm not helpless...." He stopped, and gave her a strange look. "Sure. It's you and me now, isn't it?"

A lump formed in Courtney's throat. She got him to his feet and kept an arm around him while he steadied himself. There was a nasty knot on his temple and his bottom lip had been pulped. "They beat the snot out of you."

"They tried," Gar said.

The man in the trench coat came over. "I'm Slayne. Head Warrior," he announced. "Diana told me what you whispered to her. A few of us were worried it might be a trick but I decided to come anyway."

Soren Anderson said, "I told him if he didn't, I would come alone."

"That's right, Thor," said the man in fatigues, grinning. "Claim all the credit."

"This is Robert Montoya," Slayne introduced him.

"Thor?" Gar said in confusion.

"Each of us has a code name," Slayne said, and pointed at Soren. "Thor." He pointed at Montoya. "Ricco." He tapped his own chest. "I go by Solo." He paused, then added, "Military units use codes all the time."

Sally Ann picked that moment to call out, "Hello? Two people still tied up over here!"

Montoya drew a boot knife and went to help them.

"Thank you for saving us," Courtney said.

Cradling his SMG, Slayne said, "Our pleasure. But now we have another issue. What to do with you?"

"We were hoping we could become part of your group," Courtney said.

"I know," Slayne said. "You and a lot of other people."

"So what are you saying?" Courtney said. "You save us, then leave us on our own?"

Soren Anderson said, "Were it up to me I would take you in."

"You'd take in everybody if you could," Robert Montoya said.

Soren nodded. "The god of thunder is not only the storm bringer. He has a generous heart."

"God of thunder?" Gar said.

"Don't ask," Slayne said. He scanned the bodies and gazed up at the stars and apparently came to a decision. "All right. We'll take the four of you back with us..."

"What about our dog, mister?" Sansa said. She had gone to Gaga and was hugging her.

"Oh for.....," Slayne said.

"Please," Sansa said.

"How can we refuse the appeal of so tender a child?" Soren Anderson said.

Slayne raised a hand to his nose and pinched it as if in pain. "Sure. What's one more?"

Montoya nudged Soren. "Looks like mister killing machine has a heart, after all."

They laughed.

"You people are strange," Sally Ann said.

"As I was saying," Slayne said. "We'll take you back with us. But whether you get to stay will be up to our Leader."

"God, I hope he lets us," Sally Ann said.

"You and me, both," Courtney said.

CHAPTER 33

They called themselves the Family. They called their compound the Home.

The concrete structures Courtney had seen from afar were called Blocks, and a wide open area between them was known as the Commons.

It was there that Courtney found herself, along with Gar, Sally Ann, Sansa and Gaga. And the entire Family.

Kurt Carpenter had called them together to decide the fate of Courtney and her friends.

Courtney was all too aware of the many eyes fastened on them, studying her and the others. She stood straight and held her head high, refusing to show her worry. She was scared to death they would be rejected, that they could be cast out.

More than anything in the world, Courtney wanted to be accepted by these people. To be admitted into their Home. To be safe and secure again. Or as safe as it was possible to be in a world turned into an insane asylum.

Kurt Carpenter cleared his throat. He stood with his hands clasped behind his back, his expression kindly yet somber. "Everyone!" he began. "Most of you know why this meeting has been called. These four---," and he gestured at Courtney and her companions, "seek admittance to the Home. I've explained that all of you here didn't simply show up at the drawbridge and knock to be let in."

Some of the Family smiled and grinned

Carpenter resumed. "Everyone here was admitted by invitation only. Each of you was chosen because of specific abilities or some other factor that would contribute to our mutual welfare and survival."

Courtney's dread grew. She was certain he was going to say no.

Carpenter walked in a small circle, thoughtfully regarding his listeners. "Perhaps their arrival is fortuitous. They are certainly not the first. We have only to look beyond our walls where scores more are hoping to join us."

"We can't admit everybody," a man spoke up.

"There just isn't room," a woman said.

Kurt Carpenter looked past the Blocks at a tract of woods and cabins. "True. But we are nowhere near full capacity. And our supplies are such that we could take in quite a few more without undo strain on our resources."

"What are you saying?" a man who appeared to be Native American asked.

"That perhaps I should rethink my policy," Kurt Carpenter said. He seemed to catch himself, and smiled. "Correction. *Our* policy. While I have agreed to bear the title of your Leader, all major decisions must be by consensus. Everyone must have a say. So we will take a vote. When I point at you, say yea or nay."

Carpenter turned and smiled at Courtney. "I'll go first. My vote is yea. And I'll tell you why." He pointed at her. "This young lady warned us of an impending attack. She put our welfare above the safety of herself and her friends. That shows courage, and something else." He gazed out over the Family. "It shows us that she is willing to sacrifice herself for others. It shows compassion. It shows nobility of character."

Courtney self-consciously shifted her weight from one foot to the other. In her estimation, he was making more of it than there was.

"As for the rest," Carpenter said, "the other young lady was an honors student at her high school, and the young man, I am informed, has impressed even Mr. Slayne with his ability with a revolver."

There was laughter.

"So let's take the roll," Carpenter said. He pointed at the woman named Diana.

"Yea," she said.

Carpenter pointed at Slayne, who frowned but said, "Yea."

Carpenter pointed at Soren Anderson, who thrust his hammer aloft.

"Yea, by Odin!"

At Montoya.

"Yeah."

And so it went. In the end, the tally was unanimous.

Courtney suspected that was due to Carpenter's influence. She couldn't help herself when he faced them and announced, "There you have it." She impulsively threw her arms around him and pressed her cheek to his chest. "Thank you! Thank you! Thank you!"

Family members came forward to congratulate them.

To Courtney their friendliness was a tonic. For the first time since the war broke out, she was truly and genuinely happy.

Nor was she alone. Sally Ann was beaming. Sansa had found children her own age. Gaga was being petted.

Courtney turned to Gar and clasped his hands in hers. "We did it!"

Kurt Carpenter came up to them. "Permit me to formally welcome you to the Home. I understand you went through a lot to get here."

"Did we ever," Courtney said.

Gar shrugged, and chuckled. "Piece of cake," he said.

FINI

Be on the lookout for more great reads by David Robbins!

A GIRL, THE END OF THE WORLD AND EVERYTHING

Courtney Hewitt lived a perfectly ordinary life. Then several countries let fly with nuclear missiles and chemical and biological weapons and her life was no longer ordinary. Now Courtney has chemical clouds and radiation to deal with. To say nothing of the not-so-dead who eat the living.

ANGEL U
LET THERE BE LIGHT

Armageddon is a generation away. The forces of light and darkness will clash in the ultimate battle. To prepare humankind, the angels establish a university of literal higher learning here on Earth. Enroll now---before the demons get you.

ANGEL U
DEMIGOD

Gilgamesh the Destroyer. Demon-slayer. Son of the Moon. Two parts god, one part human. He wants nothing to do with the war between Heaven and Hell. Then Gilgamesh learns that he is not who he thought he was. He is not *what* he thought he was. To learn the truth, Gilgamesh will venture where few have dared.

ENDWORLD #28
DARK DAYS

The science fiction series that sweeps its readers into a terrifying Apocalyptic future continues. The Warriors of Alpha Triad face their greatest threat yet. Their survivalist compound, the Home, has been invaded. Not by an enemy army. Not by the horrifying mutates. This time a shapeshifter is loose among the Family. Able to change into anyone at will, it is killing like there is no tomorrow.

ENDWORLD #29
THE LORDS OF KISMET

From out of the horror of World War III, a new menace is spawned, Claiming to be the gods of old, their goal is global conquest. Three Warriors are sent to bring the Lords down---but there is more to the creatures than anyone imagined.

ENDWORLD #30
SYNTHEZOIDS

The survivors of the Apocalypse have endured a lot. Mutations. Chemical toxins. Madmen. Now a new threat arises---living horrors, thanks to science gone amok.

BLOOD FEUD #2 HOUNDS OF HATE

Chace and Cassie Shannon are back. The feud between the Harkeys and the Shannons takes the twins from the hills of Arkansas to New Orleans, where Chace has a grand scheme to set them up in style. But if the Harkeys have anything to say about it, they'll be ripped to pieces.

THE WERELING

The original Horror classic. Ocean City has a lot going for it. Nice beaches. The boardwalk. Tourists. But something new is prowling Ocean City. Something that feasts on those tourists. Something that howls at the moon, and bullets can't stop. The Jersey Shore werewolf is loose.

HIT RADIO

Franco Scarvetti has a problem. His psycho son has whacked a made man. Now a rival Family is out to do the same to his son. So Big Frank comes up with a plan. He sends his lethal pride and joy to run a radio station in a small town while he tries to smooth things over. But Big Frank never read Shakespeare and he forgets that a psycho by any other name is still....a psycho.

WILDERNESS #67
THE GIFT

Evelyn King is sixteen and in love. She tricks her father and sneaks away with the warrior she loves---straight into a pack of killers.

WILDERNESS #68
SAVAGE HEARTS

Nate and Winona King thought they were doing the right thing when they rode deep into the Rockies to return a little girl to her people. But some good deeds are fraught with perils.

WILDERNESS #69
THE AVENGER

From out of the past comes a threat the King family never expects. A killer who wants an eye for an eye.

WILDERNESS #70
LOVE AND COLD STEEL

The heart wants what the heart wants. But what if your heart leads you and the one you love into danger?